# LATE LIFE

## DAN LARGENT

BLG PUBLISHING

ISBN: 978-0-578-30216-4

# DEDICATION

THIS BOOK IS DEDICATED TO COOP, CARA, CLARENCE, AND JASON. IT HAS BEEN SUCH AN HONOR TO BRING YOUR CHARACTERS TO LIFE.

# 1

"When you're newly in love, settings don't matter. You'd go anywhere, do anything, just to be in the presence of the other person. Stuff you'd normally never consider doing all of a sudden become highly anticipated events," Clarence Walters, owner of CW Security Solutions, said as he drove his most famous client sitting in the back seat of his Cadillac Escalade.

"Is that your way of sayin' that I should be more excited about going to Gabby's dance recital?" Coop asked in return, though he already knew the answer.

"Only you know that, Coop. But, you and I both know that if this dance recital was taking place last year when you and Miss Knox were first

dating, you'd have been far more optimistic sittin' in that back seat," Clarence
mused.

Coop knew he was right. In the fall of 2006, Coop would've been
excited to accompany Cara to a paint-drying exhibit, yet there he was dreading
the next three hours that awaited him. It wasn't that he didn't want to be
supportive of Gabby. He adored her, and she him.

However, Coop had finally worked himself back into Cleveland's
starting rotation after having Tommy John surgery, and the club was poised to
make a run at the 2007 playoffs. They had just returned earlier that morning on
a red-eye flight after a 14-game East Coast swing and Coop was scheduled to
pitch the next day. Despite his love for Gabby, not to mention Cara and her
family, Coop really wanted to make sure that he was well-rested for his first
home start since his return. The thought of sitting in an uncomfortable metal
folding chair wasn't exactly what he had in mind for his one night off.

Coop's cell phone chirped to life and he looked at the display. It was
Cara and he didn't need to answer the call to know why she was calling, but he
opened up the Motorola Razr and answered nonetheless.

"Yes, Cara, I'm on my way," Coop said in a sarcastic tone.

"That's not why I'm calling," Cara replied in a panicked tone. "It's my dad…"

She was unable to finish her sentence, and Coop could hear her begin to sob on the other end of the line.

"Charlie?" Coop asked, referring to Cara's father. "Cara, what's the matter?"

Coop knew that it could be a number of things. Charlie Knox has been confined to a wheelchair for the past decade after an accident while working at the Ford plant. In addition to being paralyzed from the waist down, he had also battled depression and a number of physical ailments related to the injury.

"Mom went to wake him up from his nap…" Cara managed to say between sobs, "but, she… He wouldn't wake-up…"

Coop's heart sank as Cara continued.

"He was barely breathing, but she couldn't get him to wake-up…"

"Oh, Lord, Cara… I'm so sorry," Coop said, trying to find the right words. "Where are you now?"

"Mom called 9-1-1 and they just took him to Metro in an ambulance. Mom rode with him and I'm driving her car there now. Coop, I'm scared…"

"I know, but your daddy's a fighter, Cara. Try to stay positive," Coop replied doing his best to reassure her. "I'll meet you guys there. Is there anything I can do to help?"

"Just come… I'm so scared."

"Did you call your brothers?"

"Not yet… I called you first. Oh God, Jason and Johnny are already at Gabby's recital. Should I call them now? What should I do?" Cara pleaded.

"You don't worry about that. I'll call your brothers. You just worry about driving safely to the hospital, and I'll meet you there, okay?"

"Okay…" Cara answered and Coop could hear her trying to control the sobs that were doing their best to reach a crescendo.

"I'll be there soon. I love you," Coop reassured.

"Love you, too…" Cara managed to reply before ending the call.

Coop was pretty sure that he heard Cara finally let out the sobs that she had been trying to stifle just before the call ended. His mind began to cycle through the varying options available to him as to how he would let Cara's brothers know about their dad's condition - none of which were ideal, especially for Jason who was probably wondering why nobody had shown up yet to his daughter's recital.

"What's goin' on, Coop? Is something wrong with Mr. Knox?" Clarence's inquiry snapped Coop back to the present.

"Oh, sorry..." Coop answered. "We need to go to Metro, Clarence. Joanne couldn't wake him up from his nap."

"Oh Lord," Clarence said before he began reciting a prayer out loud on Charlie's behalf.

Coop tried calling Christopher first. Christopher was currently stationed in Japan with the Navy, where Coop figured it would be early morning and he might be able to get ahold of him. Though, with Christopher, one never knew as he worked unconventional hours doing an even more unconventional job that he wasn't even allowed to talk about.

Still, Christopher was the best bet to call first. Cara's other two older brothers, Jason and Johnny, were likely together at Gabby's recital already and Coop still wasn't sure what the best way was going to be to tell them.

"Is this THE Cooper Madison calling my phone at 7 o'clock in the morning?" Christopher answered, his voice dripping with manufactured excitement, which only made what Coop was going to tell him next that much harder.

"Hey, bud…" Coop paused as he tried to find the right words.

"Coop? Is everything alright?" Christopher asked.

"It's your dad, Christopher…"

The second oldest of Cara's trio of elder male siblings took the news as one would expect of a career military man. Coop could almost hear him swallow down any emotion that may have been trying to escape before responding in a calm, controlled manner. He wanted to make sure his mom was okay and if Coop could give any insight into the severity of his father's condition.

"I honestly don't know," Coop had responded, "but I think you should come home, if possible, Christopher."

"Yeah, of course," he replied. "I'll get on the first bird out of here. Might take a day or two before I'm home though. I'll call you when I know for sure and I'll have my cell phone with me. Just keep me updated, okay?"

"I'm sure your momma and Cara will be happy to hear that. You can call me anytime, too."

# 2

Cooper Madison's confident strides betrayed the trepidation that consumed him as he approached the Emergency Room lobby at MetroHealth Medical Center. He wanted to be a pillar of strength for whatever awaited Cara and her family, but he also could feel the memories of his own father's sudden death creeping into his thoughts, especially after his phone call to Christopher.

As Coop was making that first phone call, Clarence took it upon himself to call Grace Brooks, one of the other bodyguards at CW Security Solutions, who happened to be at the recital with the rest of Cara's family. While she had worked security details in the past for the Knox family, on this night she was actually attending as Johnny's plus one.

It was while attending Coop's first game in Cleveland that Johnny, a personal trainer and drug-free bodybuilder, had successfully convinced Grace to join him for a workout session at his gym. Grace, who in addition to working for Clarence was also an up-and-coming MMA fighter, agreed to attend one session - even though she assumed he was just another meathead like the countless others she encountered at the gym.

During that session, Grace saw Johnny as more than just a typical muscle-bound trainer, most of whom she had determined must suffer from Peter Pan syndrome, but rather as a young man who was insanely passionate about what he believed. Grace appreciated that level of dedication and began to view Johnny as a kindred spirit. It didn't hurt that he had kind eyes, a flawless physique, and that he was slightly taller than she was at just over 6 feet in height.

One session turned into two, and soon they were training together five days a week. It took Johnny almost a month to ask her out to dinner, and he felt foolish when Grace's response was, "It's about damn time, Knox!"

The pair had become quite serious in the months since, and Johnny had officially become Grace's trainer as she prepared for her first MMA fight, which was scheduled two months later in early December. Grace had now become a fixture at all Knox family gatherings, which included that evening's recital.

Jason and Erica had already been waiting inside the venue and were saving seats for the rest of the group while she and Johnny stood outside Gabby's recital to greet Coop and Cara when Clarence's call came.

Johnny could tell something wasn't right as he studied Grace's reaction to the call and after she thanked Clarence and ended the call, she informed him of the news about Charlie.

"What do you think we should do? We have to tell Jason now, right?" Johnny asked, his voice trembling.

"I think we have to," Grace agreed. "Clarence said that there really isn't anything we can do right now besides sitting in the waiting room at the hospital. I think we should let Jason make that decision. Do you want me to go in and tell him?"

"No, I'll go inside and let him know. Can you pull your truck around? I'll tell him that you and I will go now, and maybe he can leave right after Gabby is done on stage."

"Absolutely, and tell Jason that I'll call Clarence and have him pick Erica and Gabby up after the recital," Grace said before giving Johnny a long hug. She could feel him fighting back his emotions as he squeezed her tight in return.

"Thank you," he whispered as he kissed her on the cheek.

A few minutes later Johnny appeared from the building's entrance, alone. As he walked towards the passenger side of the SUV, Grace could see that tears were in his eyes.

"Jason said that he's going to meet us at Metro as soon as Gabby is off the stage," Johnny informed as he sat next to Grace.

"Okay," Grace replied as she reached over and placed her hand on his cheek. "Clarence said that he just dropped Coop off and is already heading this way to join them inside."

"Thank you," Johnny answered, tears now streaming down his face as he looked out the passenger window. "Did anyone call Christopher yet?"

"Coop did. He's going to get on the next flight out of Japan and hopefully will be here in the next day or so," Grace reassured.

"Good," was all Johnny said in return as Grace put the SUV into drive.

Coop saw Joanne and Cara sitting in the waiting room before they noticed him enter. Joanne had her head in her hands, while Cara sat beside her with her arm draped over her mother's shoulders. She had a vacant look on her face and her eyes were puffy from crying.

Coop took a deep breath, steeled himself, and approached them.

"I got here as soon as I could," Coop said as they both looked up at him. Cara immediately stood and wrapped her arms around him as a wave of emotion consumed her.

"I'm so happy you're here," Cara managed to say as he pulled her head to his chest.

"Me too," he replied, before directing his attention to Joanne as he continued to hold Cara. "I called Christopher and he is going to get back here as soon as possible, and Clarence is making sure that Johnny and Jason know. Is there anything else I can do to help, Miz Knox? I'm so sorry…"

"I… I don't think so, Cooper," Joanne replied, forcing a smile as she looked up at him. "I just feel so awful about missing Gabby's recital…"

"She'll understand, I promise," Coop reassured. "Have y'all heard anything from the doctors yet?"

"No," Cara answered. "Nothing since they told us that they were taking him back. I'm so scared…"

Joanne, her elbows pressed into her thighs, buried her face back into her palms and began to sob. Cara, upon hearing her mother, pressed her cheek firmly against Coop's broad chest and followed suit.

Coop closed his eyes, pulled Cara tight, and said a prayer for Charlie.

# 3

A flash of lightning briefly transformed the night sky, providing a glimpse of artificial daylight before the crack of thunder that followed shook the windows lining the entrance to MetroHealth's Emergency Room lobby.

Cooper Madison stared out into the darkness and tried to steady the thoughts racing through his head. Three hours had passed since his arrival, and aside from a brief visit from the nurse manager to tell the family that Charlie was still in surgery, there hadn't been any updates on his condition.

Cara, perhaps in an effort to escape the sadness that had seemingly enveloped the waiting room, took her mom for a walk to the hospital cafeteria. Joanne protested at first, but Cara had convinced her that a cup of coffee was in order.

"You need to go home and sleep," Jason said, startling Coop. "You think any of the Boston batters are still up?"

"Actually, I'm betting most of them are. Those guys really like strip clubs," Coop laughed, returning his gaze to the storm outside.

"Don't I know it," Jason sighed. "Back when I was still a beat cop, I used to see quite a few of my favorite ballplayers out on the streets until the wee hours of the morning. Had to give a lot of courtesy rides back to the team hotel and even keep a few of their names out of the headlines, if you catch my drift."

"Preaching to the choir, Detective. I've been driven back to the team hotel by some of the best cops in cities all across America. But, those days are long passed. Thank God…"

"In all seriousness though, Coop. Go home. Get some rest. Cara will understand," Jason said, punctuating his words for effect. "You have worked too hard to get back out there on the mound, and I can't let you sit in a hospital all night when you are scheduled to pitch in less than 24 hours."

"I don't know, Jason…"

"Well, I do. Besides, I may or may not have a hundo riding on you," Jason let his words hang, knowing that after what happened to Pete Rose, that the one thing ballplayers do not want to be associated with is gambling on baseball.

"Bullshit," Coop scoffed, not taking the bait. "Erica would never let you bet that much on a game."

"Well, you got me there," Jason admitted. "But, my advice is still the same. Go home, Coop. If I have to cuff you and throw you in the back of the cruiser, I will gladly abuse my authority as an officer to do so…"

"You should go…"

Cara's voice had startled Coop and he turned away from the window to find her standing behind Jason, styrofoam cup of coffee in hand.

"Cara, I don't think that's necessary," Coop protested. "I can sleep on one of the sofas if I need to."

"Coop, you're twice the size of the biggest couch here. Don't be ridiculous," Cara replied. "Go home. You've worked too hard. We'll be fine. I promise."

Coop looked to Jason.

"Don't look at me, she's right," Jason laughed.

"Okay, but only if you promise to call me if something changes with your daddy," Coop relented, before reiterating his terms. "Please. Promise me that you'll call?"

"I promise," Cara said as she walked into his already outstretched arms, which enveloped her petite frame in a comforting squeeze, her face buried in his broad chest.

"Are you sure about this?" Coop whispered, his cheek resting just above her ear.

"Positive..."

"I'll go let Grace know that you're leaving," Jason said before walking away.

While Grace was ultimately there to support Johnny, she was always "On the clock" as an employee of CW Security Solutions when it came to Cooper Madison, as he was their highest profile client, not to mention the catalyst for their company's booming growth.

In the months since Coop had retained their services, Clarence's small security firm had grown exponentially as every high profile athlete, businessman, and visiting celebrities looking for peace of mind had flooded his office with requests. This sudden surge in clients had enabled Clarence to hire a dozen new security guards, all of whom were either former cops or discharged military personnel.

The only thing that hadn't changed for CW Security Solutions was that Cooper Madison was their number one priority, and only Clarence and Grace were permitted to work on his security detail, which was a 24/7 on-call job that Coop paid top-dollar for.

"You ready?" Grace asked Coop, who was still holding Cara in the same spot where Jason had left them minutes earlier.

"Yes, ma'am," Coop answered with a half-smile.

"Go home, and promise me you'll get some sleep," Cara implored before giving him a soft kiss on the cheek.

"I love you," Coop whispered, his forehead resting on hers, their eyes locked.

"I love you more…"

*Late Life*

# 4

On the one year anniversary since Vivian Tong's body had washed up on the shore of Lake Erie's Edgewater Beach, the man known to Cleveland law enforcement as Eugene Lankford honored her memory by raising his vodka and cranberry in a silent toast. While her murder had been deemed the work of Cleveland's notorious Edgewater Park Killer, the man who was actually responsible for her death had just paid her a tribute while sitting alone at a table inside Sokolowski's University Inn.

The EPK murders had first gripped the city two years earlier when Stoya Fedorov's body was found along the banks of Cleveland's Edgewater Park - arguably the Great Lake's most prominent public beach.

Fedorov, an undocumented Russian working as a prostitute for the Russian mob, was the first of three victims to be discovered at Edgewater in

2005. The bodies of two more Russian women followed shortly after hers, and with them came the paranoia that the city of Cleveland had a serial killer on the loose.

Authorities would later learn in the fall of 2006 that an unassuming used car salesman name Ernie Page was the man responsible for the Fedorov murder. Thanks to the police work of Detective Jason Knox and Commander Mick McCarthy, Page confessed to strangling the Russian in a cheap motel room, though he steadfastly denied any involvement in the deaths of the other two women all the way up until the moment he put a bullet into his head.

Horace "HoJo" Johnston, Cleveland's Chief of Police at the time, was far more interested in grabbing headlines than he was for finding the truth. It came as no surprise when, despite having anything other than circumstantial evidence connecting Ernie Page to the other murders, HoJo deemed the EPK case as being closed.

While the unassuming public rejoiced in the thought that they no longer had to worry about a serial killer walking the streets of Cleveland, those within the department and even some members of the media remained less than convinced.

HoJo had barely been able to enjoy a victory lap by the time Vivian Tong's lifeless body was discovered at Edgewater. Despite the fact that the initials "EPK" had been carved into her chest, HoJo had done everything in his power to keep that part of the story out of the headlines. The Chief had already declared Ernie Page as the EPK on every television talk show that called, and the last thing that he needed was to admit that his department had dropped the ball.

It was during Knox and McCarthy's initial investigation into Vivian Tong's murder when the name Eugene Lankford first appeared as a possible suspect, though only those close to the case would ever have heard it.

Described by witnesses as a middle-aged, bald, white man, Lankford had been the last person seen with Vivian Tong before her disappearance. Tong, a stripper at Buddy's Speakeasy, had developed a reputation for taking customers like Lankford back to her apartment for more intimate encounters. Aside from the bogus West Virginia driver's license he used to gain entry into the club, nothing more was ever found in regards to Eugene Lankford.

Any doubts by those in the department that the serial killer was still alive were vanquished the day that HoJo was found strangled to death inside his car, with the initials "EPK" carved into his chest. The killer had used an industrial zip tie to do the job, and this time he left a note at the crime scene.

The killer claimed in his letter, which was addressed to Detective Knox, that it was he, and not Ernie Page, that was the true EPK. The note went on to promise that there would be more victims, especially if Jason and his fellow officers did not clean up the corruption inside the city's police department.

Days later, the EPK followed through on his promise when the body of Vance Gold, owner of Buddy's Speakeasy, was discovered on the floor of his club. Gold, like HoJo, had been strangled to death by the same type of industrial zip tie.

The EPK was getting bolder in his tactics, managing to kill the strip club owner despite the fact that there had been two police officers watching the place. This time, instead of a note, a photograph of a 13 year old girl named Jane had been left next to Vance Gold's body.

That photograph eventually led to the identification of a man named Phil Worthington, whose daughter had died at the age of 18 of a drug overdose while working as a prostitute for none other than Vance Gold.

Worthington, a retired truck driver who had spent the years following his daughter's death running a small fishing charter out of Edgewater's marina, was soon linked to the deaths of HoJo, Gold, and the other two Russian women who had been found on the same beach as Stoya Fedorov.

Detective Knox finally had an identity for the real EPK, but before he could close the case, Phil Worthington's body had been found stabbed to death inside a Gatlinburg, Tennessee motel room.

While the authorities had assured the general public that the EPK had died when Phil Worthington was found inside that motel room, they had also never been able to prove that he had anything to do with the Tong murder.

Sure, she had "EPK" carved into her chest, but that's the only place where any connection to Phil existed, and it was easier to just let the case go cold than to chase a ghost.

That was just fine with the man that enjoyed a plate of Sokolowski's famous pierogies, because he knew that authorities believed that Eugene Lankford had vanished the very moment that Vivian Tong took her last breath.

*Late Life*

However, the man who had assumed that identity was still very much alive, and he had killed again.

# 5

*Thwap!*

The sweet sound of Cooper Madison's final warm-up pitch as it popped into the soft leather grain of veteran catcher Chaz DeLisio's mitt served notice to anyone within earshot that Coop was back at full strength. It had been a long, arduous journey since undergoing Tommy John surgery, but he was back where he belonged as a starting pitcher in the majors.

"Hey, big guy," Chaz said as he approached the mound. "I'd ask you if you're ready for this, but my hand hurts too much from your pitches to bother..."

"Feeling good, CD," Coop replied, talking into his glove as was customary for any pitcher as he spoke while on the field of play.

"Ok, remember, we're gonna work the first three guys backward, then nothing but heavy gas to start off four through nine," Chaz said, also into his mitt. Throwing off-speed pitches to Detroit's first three batters, according to the scouting report, was the best approach as all three loved to swing at first pitch fastballs.

"Yessir. You just put those ugly fingers of yours down and I'll do whatever they tell me to," Coop answered. Coop always pitched best when he put his trust in the catcher to call a good game, and only a few were better at that than Chaz DeLisio.

"Atta boy," Chaz said as he gave Coop a pat on the rear before jogging back towards home plate.

Coop walked to the back of the pitcher's mound and squatted down to carve the initials "LB" into the dirt with his finger, a ritual that he had done throughout his career as a tribute to his late friend, Lane Bixby.

Lane, who had been one of the best athletes that Coop had ever played with during his high school years, passed away from Acute Lymphoblastic Leukemia at the age of 17. His death had made a profound impact on Coop, and carving those initials in the dirt before every game was his way of letting Lane know that he would never be forgotten.

"Lane, if you're watching like you said you would, I could use some of that divine intervention right about now," Coop whispered into his glove as he looked upwards towards the heavens.

While he did manage to get a few hours of sleep after leaving the hospital, his body could have used twice as much. He had called Cara immediately after waking up and learned that Charlie was out of surgery, but far from being out of the woods.

Cara relayed what the surgeon, Dr. Kathryn Dye, had told the family after the procedure. Charlie had sustained a massive heart attack, and while the EMT's had managed to revive him in the ambulance on the way to MetroHealth Medical Center, Dr. Dye had to perform a quadruple bypass to ensure that his heart would function properly going forward.

"Well, that's good news, right?" Coop had asked in regards to the successful bypass operation.

"Sort of," Cara replied, but the emotion in her voice foreshadowed that what she was about to say next was anything but good news. She tried to speak, but couldn't.

"What is it, Cara?" Coop asked.

"They said that because he was unconscious for so long and his brain wasn't getting any oxygen, that there's a good chance that he's…"

Coop didn't need her to finish the sentence to know what Charlie's next battle would be. He knew that the longer the brain doesn't get oxygen the greater the likelihood is that Charlie suffered brain damage. The only question was, if that was the case, just how severe the damage would be.

"I'm so sorry, Cara," Coop said, angry with himself for not being there when Cara got the news. "I should've been there…"

"Please, don't say that," she replied. "This has been hard enough on all of us. I can't deal with you feeling guilty for doing what you needed to do, Coop."

They both let a few seconds of silence pass before Coop finally spoke.

"Listen, I'm gonna hop in the shower and swing by the hospital before I head to the ball park. Can I bring you anything? Fresh clothes? Tooth brush? Food? Coffee?"

"Just bring yourself," Cara answered. "I'm planning on going home when you leave for the ballpark, anyway."

"Fair enough. I should be there in less than an hour, okay?"

"Hey, Coop?" Cara asked.

"What's up?"

"Are you going to be upset if I'm not at the game tonight? The doctor said that they're hoping to run some tests to measure brain activity later today, and I really want to be here for my mom."

"Are you kidding me? Of course not," Coop reassured her. "Heck, I'd be mad if you did come."

"Nothing…" Cara said. The term had been the couple's codeword for saying everything that they couldn't put into words otherwise.

"Nothing…" Coop replied.


"Play ball!"

*Late Life*

The booming voice of the home plate umpire, Nino Bova, snapped Coop back to reality. The previous evening's storm had given way to a perfectly mild evening in Cleveland, and the sellout crowd at Jacobs Field was hoping to witness a triumphant return to the greatness that was Cooper Madison.

Coop toed the rubber, and glared at the leadoff batter, Logan Atkins. Chaz DeLisio put two fingers down, calling for a slider away. Coop nodded and came to his set, took a deep breath, and then rocked back and fired.

# 6

Everyone in the private hospitality suite at MetroHealth Medical Center cheered as they watched Cooper Madison retire the side in order during the first inning of play.

The hospitality suite had an array of couches, tables, and chairs for the family to relax in as they waited for updates on Charlie's progress. Most prominently, was the large flatscreen TV in the corner of the room. It was tuned in to Coop's game in an effort to give everyone in the room a brief escape from the reality of their situation.

Cara sat front and center, living and dying with each pitch that Coop threw. She was so proud of him and couldn't contain the tears of joy that streamed down her face after he recorded that last out.

*Late Life*

Better yet, for Cara, was that Coop fulfilled his promise to her when he used his hand to make the letter "C" and place it over his heart for the camera as he walked off the field at the end of the inning. Earlier, when Coop was at the hospital, he told Cara to make sure she was watching him as he walked to the dugout after each inning, regardless of how he pitched.

"What are you going to do?" Cara had asked him as they each sipped a cup of coffee in the hospital cafeteria.

"You'll know it when you see it," Coop replied, slyly. "Let's just say it will be for both you and your daddy, so you know that you're both there with me tonight."

When the game came back on after the commercial break, the announcers talked over a replay of Coop walking off the field.

"*Many of you at home might be wondering just what that gesture means that Cooper Madison made over his chest as he walked off the field,*" the play-by-play announcer said. "*Well, folks, Cooper Madison made sure to tell our crew before the game tonight that he would be honoring both his girlfriend, Cara Knox, and her father Charlie, who we are told is currently dealing with a medical situation. While Coop wouldn't elaborate exactly what*

32

*Mr. Knox was going through, he did want us to make sure we had a camera on him after each inning tonight. So, Charlie, Cara, and the rest of the Knox family, everyone here in the broadcast booth would also like to send well-wishes for a speedy recovery...*"

"Oh my Lord," Joanne Knox said standing up and speaking above a whisper for the first time in two days. "They just said Charlie's name on the television! Did you all hear that?"

Seeing Joanne display some life for the first time since arriving at the hospital did nothing to help Cara suppress the tears that were already flowing. She was positive that in that very moment she had never loved Coop more.

Cara's family had been in a slightly better, yet guarded, frame of mind since their last update from the doctors. Charlie had been moved to the ICU, and after the team of doctors that met with the family to explain what exactly a hypoxic-ischemic coma was, they also informed the family of a procedure called therapeutic hypothermia, which they had started to use on Charlie almost immediately after the surgery.

"Therapeutic hypothermia can be a good thing if, like Charlie, the heart was restarted but he was still not responsive," Dr. Dye had informed. "It can raise the chance that Charlie will wake up. Basically, we are keeping his body temperature at around 89 degrees over the next 18-24 hours in hopes that it will reduce the chances of brain damage."

"How exactly does keeping his body cold help reduce the chances of brain damage?" Jason inquired.

"To be honest," Dr. Dye replied, "we don't really know the exact reason, but recent studies have shown that patients who receive this type of treatment after cardiac arrest have a much better prognosis for regaining brain function. I can't stress enough how important the next 24 hours will be for Charlie, and the best thing that all of you can do is to continue to stay positive, which is why I'd like to introduce you to one of our hospital chaplains, Marsha Beeching."

The petite woman Dr. Dye gestured to appeared to be in her mid to late 50's. She had short salt and pepper hair, along with a welcoming smile and caring eyes. Her clothing would easily have her confused with being a librarian, secretary, or high school guidance counselor, rather than a member of the hospital clergy.

"It's a pleasure to meet all of you," Marsha said, as she made sure to shake each family member's hand and ask for their names.

She had been a staff chaplain at MetroHealth for over a decade after earning her Master of Divinity degree from Franciscan University in Steubenville, Ohio, and completing a residency in Clinical Pastoral Education at the VA hospital in Akron.

Marsha had seen just about everything during her time at MetroHealth and she had become an expert at making an immediate, personal connection with every family she met. She had spent the following two hours after being introduced to the Knox family listening to them express their concerns, answering whatever questions they had to the best of her ability, and even holding Joanne's hand as the two women prayed together.

As promised, Marsha had even returned after her shift at the hospital was over to join the family as they watched Coop pitch on television while they all enjoyed pizza courtesy of Stucky's Place.

Stucky, the owner, was one of Charlie's oldest friends from their days working together at the Ford Plant in Brook Park. He had always looked out for the Knox family after the accident that had left Charlie confined to a wheelchair, even giving Cara a job as she paid her way through college at

Cleveland State. It was while working for Stucky that she met Coop, and as

Cara took a bite of pepperoni pizza, she couldn't help but feel some comfort in

it all.

# 7

Cooper Madison sat on a metal folding chair in front of his locker inside the clubhouse at Jacobs Field using the white towel that was draped around his neck to blot his damp hair as he simultaneously answered questions from the small crowd of reporters that had descended upon him. He had just pitched 7 strong innings in his first game back in Cleveland's starting rotation, scattering 5 hits and striking out 11 batters while earning the 4 to 1 win over Detroit. Aside from the solo home run that he gave up to start the 5th inning, he felt as if it was as good of an outcome as he could have asked for.

"Coop," began one of the reporters, "your fastball was clocked as high as 98 miles per hour in the 7th tonight, which was actually harder than you threw in any of the first 6 innings. Do you feel as though you could've gone back out there for the 8th?"

"Yessir," Coop replied. "I think any pitcher will tell y'all that they always want to go back out there, especially when they're feeling it like I was tonight. But, I also know that I'm on a pretty strict pitch count at this point, so I understand why we went to the bullpen."

"Can you tell us more about the gesture you made at the end of each inning for your girlfriend, Cara, and her father, Charlie Knox?" asked another reporter.

"I was just letting some very special people know that I was thinking about them," Coop answered. "I know y'all can appreciate me not going into any more specifics than that."

Coop spent the next ten minutes answering the reporters' questions, all of whom respected his wishes and stuck to the usual post game inquiries. Afterwards, he showered and changed as quickly as he could so that he could head over to the hospital to join Cara and her family.

Clarence had just gotten off the phone with Cara's brother, Jason, when Coop emerged from the stadium. While other members of the CW Security Solutions team would routinely perform security detail for the Knox family, it was Clarence who drove their top client - almost exclusively.

The fact that Jason would call Clarence with an update on Charlie's health, instead of Coop himself, wasn't out of the norm. After all, it was Jason who had originally reached out to Clarence when his sister and her famous new boyfriend were in need of a security detail, as the two had worked together for the CPD prior to Clarence's retirement.

"Nice job out there tonight, young man," Clarence said as he opened the door to his SUV for Coop.

"Thank ya kindly, Clarence. Chaz called a great game behind the plate tonight. Made my job easy," Coop replied.

Once he was back behind the wheel in his SUV, Clarence took a deep breath before relaying Jason's update to Coop. "Jason called me just before you came out," Clarence said, looking back at Coop in the rear view mirror.

"What'd he have to say? Is everything okay?" Coop asked, meeting Clarence's eyes in the reflection.

"To be honest," Clarence began, "Jason said that the doctors aren't really sure. Apparently, they met with the family a little bit ago and said that the next 24 hours will be the most important to determine what level of brain activity he still has. So, it's a waiting game..."

"Did Jason say how Cara's holding up?"

"She's hanging in there. Everyone is. I think they're all just trying to stay as positive as they can…"

Coop just nodded in response and Clarence could see the concern on his face. He had started to work for Coop when their relationship was just beginning and had helped see them through more ups and downs over the past year than most couples have in a lifetime .

"One thing is for sure though, Coop," Clarence spoke, breaking the brief silence.

"What's that?"

"You gave the whole family a reason to be hopeful tonight out there on that mound. I guess they had quite the watch party going on in that hospitality suite. What you did tonight, overcoming your own obstacles, was inspiring, Coop."

"I'd hardly call throwing a baseball after arm surgery inspiring when you compare it to what Charlie's dealing with," Coop sighed.

"Inspiration doesn't have a sliding scale, Coop," Clarence countered. "People can find inspiration anywhere, man, and what you did tonight was nothing short of inspirational. Not just for Cara and her family, but for anyone out there who's trying to overcome adversity. Don't sell yourself short, but more importantly, don't forget the power you have to make a difference…"

"I suppose you're right," Coop said, before adding with a wry smile, "As always…"

Coop had grown to love the man tasked with his safety, and there was no sarcasm at all in his last words to Clarence. While he would often tease Clarence that he could be the next Dr. Phil - only way cooler - he truly cherished their relationship and the advice that Clarence would give him.

As Clarence's SUV headed southwest out of the player's parking lot onto Carnegie Avenue, Jason's phone buzzed to life as he was waiting for them to arrive at the hospital. The name on the caller ID wasn't unfamiliar to him in the least bit, but it had been months since the two had spoken.

*Late Life*

# 8

"Detective Knox, I'm so glad I was able to get ahold of you," Hannah LaMarca said before adding, "I heard about your father and I just wanted you to know if you need anything, I'm only a phone call away."

"I appreciate that," Jason replied. "It's been a long few days."

"I bet…"

"How are things going at Channel One?" Jason changed the subject, not quite ready to have a back and forth about his dad.

"Well, I didn't expect to be at the anchor desk this soon," Hannah responded, "but, I'm not complaining…"

Just a few months earlier, Hannah's exclusive five part series on the Edgewater Park Killer had not only won her a second local Emmy, but the story was also picked up by Dateline NBC. After Keith Morrison's two hour feature aired, that prominently featured Hannah, her popularity in Cleveland had achieved a meteoric rise unlike anything ever seen before.

Channel One executives, who had already restructured her contract once in an effort to keep her from going to a bigger market, gave her an extension that contained something far more valuable to her than the pay raise that accompanied it: weekday anchor of the evening news.

"So, how long before you're on the network news?" Jason asked, only half kidding.

"I'm right where I want to be," Hannah chuckled.

"That's the crazy thing about growing up in Cleveland," Jason replied. "You spend most of your childhood trying to figure out the best way to leave this town, only to realize when you're older that you don't want to."

"That is so true," agreed Hannah.

Jason, sensing that there was obviously another reason for Hannah's call, asked, "Did you need something else, Miss LaMarca?"

"Guilty," Hannah confirmed.

"Go on…"

"Have you ever heard of Bryce Canyon National Park?" Hannah asked.

"Can't say that I have," Jason replied. "Why do you ask?"

"So, nobody contacted you this week regarding Bryce Canyon?"

"I have no clue where you're going with this," Jason responded, confused.

Hannah informed, "I have it on good authority that a middle-aged woman's body, or what was left of it, was discovered in that park earlier this week."

"I don't even know where Bryce Canyon is," Jason mused. "Not to mention, even if I did, I have no idea why that would concern me."

"It's in southern Utah," said Hannah. "About a 4 hour drive from Vegas, but that's not as important as what was found with the body."

"Okay, I'll bite…"

"The remains apparently had an industrial zip-tie around the neck, and a serrated buck knife was lodged into what was left of the chest cavity…"

Jason felt a chill run down his spine as Hannah purposely let her words hang for a long pause; however, he failed to fill the void.

"You still there, Detective?" she prompted.

"Sorry... Yeah, I'm here," Jason answered, rejoining the conversation. "How long did they say the body had been there?"

"Hard to tell until the coroner's report, but they are guessing at least 6 to 8 months. Maybe even longer..."

"You don't really think Dolly did this, do you?" Jason asked, knowing that the young reporter was obviously hoping for some sort of connection to the case that had helped launch her career. "That would be one hell of a conclusion to jump to."

Dolly Barnes, otherwise known to the media as "Deadly Dolly" had been on the run since the murders of the last two men she was seen with - Lance Barnes in Buffalo, New York and Phil Worthington in Gatlinburg, Tennessee.

DNA tests from each of the crime scenes had confirmed that the same woman had been at both crime scenes, but whoever that female was had no previous DNA records on file. Authorities believed if they could locate and arrest Dolly and get a DNA sample, that it would further prove their already strong circumstantial case against the elusive Black Widow.

"Deadly Dolly" had become a household name since her likely involvement in the murder of the infamous EPK killer, Phil Worthington, and she was featured on Dateline NBC. Surveillance video images of Dolly in Gatlinburg, along with the picture on her fake driver's license, had been splashed all over the news for months.

Dolly sightings were being reported from all over the world in the days following the popular crime program. The most credible ones had her heading west in the days following Phil Worthington's murder, as his truck was left abandoned 230 miles to the west of Gatlinburg just outside Nashville along Interstate 40.

Earlier on in the investigation, a used car salesman in Bellevue, Tennessee, came forward after realizing he had likely sold a car to the curvy blonde fugitive. The salesman had not violated any laws by selling a 1998 Buick Century to the woman who said her name was June without getting any sort of identification from her, because he was not required to for any car costing less than $10,000.

It was a straight cash purchase, and the woman had informed him that she already had plates that she would transfer on her own. When he offered to help her put the license plate on the rear of the vehicle, she declined and said she had it covered as she produced a screwdriver and what appeared to be an Ohio license plate.

She thanked him for his help and waited until he went back inside the small office, which was really just a double-wide trailer plopped down in the middle of the lot, to quickly screw the plate on the rear of the sedan before speeding away. It wasn't until the next day that the salesman had realized who the woman likely was, and it took him another day after that before contacting police to come forward, as he wanted to make sure with his attorney that he had not done anything illegal in the sale of the vehicle.

Meanwhile, Dolly had been given a two day head start. As more and more news reports were telling viewers to be on the lookout for a blonde woman, around 50 years of age, driving a 1998 Buick Century, law enforcement fully expected Dolly to have already changed her hair color and vehicle by the time those reports aired.

Even after the resurgence of Dolly sightings following the Dateline episode, the federal law enforcement officers who had taken over the case were no closer to finding Deadly Dolly than they were when she fled

Gatlinburg. It was as if she vanished off the radar, prompting many law enforcement officers, like Jason, to assume that she was laying low and living off of Phil's cash.

"No, I don't think Dolly did this," Hannah replied.

"Good, because I was just about to go full detective mode on you and explain that the zip-tie wasn't even part of Dolly's M-0."

"Right. Neither was killing women," Hannah agreed.

"Then why would I care about this case at all? Help me out here, Miss LaMarca," Jason sighed.

"Because, I think the body *is* Dolly…"

"Get the hell outta here!" Jason laughed incredulously. "That's quite a stretch, even for a member of the media, Miss LaMarca! Just because a middle-aged woman's body is found in a park with a knife and a plastic zip-tie?"

Hannah had fully anticipated that Jason would respond the way he did, which is why she let him enjoy his moment before dropping the hammer on him. The pair had always enjoyed a mostly respectful working relationship, but they also loved to compete with each other, especially when it came to the most valuable commodity in both of their professions: information.

"Oh, I almost forgot one small piece of information," Hannah said, coyly. "The buck knife was apparently of the souvenir variety. I'm told that it said 'Gatlinburg' on the handle…"

# 9

The man known as Eugene Lankford had not planned to kill again. He was smart enough to know just how fortunate he was that his first victim's murder had been attributed to a man who had never even met her.

Only those working the case knew that Phil Worthington likely didn't kill Vivian, and they were no closer to finding the man from that West Virginia driver's license, either.

While he was certain that the lead detective working the case would forever be on the lookout for the mysterious Eugene Lankford, he was just as certain that he would never find him.

The man truly believed that he never would have killed the first time had his victim just gone along with the plan. After all, it's what he had paid her hundreds of dollars for.

Vivian Tong, however, had tried to go back on her word.

The dancer turned prostitute had always been so cooperative in regards to playing his sexual games during their encounters in the fall of 2007, that it had caught him off guard when she refused to stick to the script. Her sudden defiance temporarily removed the power that he had held over her, but in a rage he quickly shifted the balance back in his favor via a backhand across her right temple.

The blow had launched Vivian's petite frame into the side of his car, causing her head to snap back on impact before her body slid down the driver's side door and onto a paved street outside her apartment building in Cleveland's Clark-Fulton neighborhood. He looked around to see if anyone may have witnessed the violent blow, but it was well after two o'clock in the morning and every window facing the street was dark.

Regardless, even if someone had seen him hit her, the chances of them ever saying anything were slim to none. Snitches were not welcome in this part of town, which had been overrun by gangs, drugs, and violent crimes during the past decade.

Vivian had begun to moan on the ground as she regained consciousness, so he quickly kneeled down and placed his left hand over her mouth to shut her up. That only made things worse for him as she began to squirm and kick, so he took his right hand and grabbed her by the throat. The more she fought, the harder he squeezed, pressing the back of her head to the pavement and putting his knee on her chest.

As her ability to fight back slowly slipped away, with it went any doubt in his mind that he would have to finish the job as he had crossed the point of no return. This would no longer be viewed as an assault - it was now attempted murder.

The thought of her almond-shaped eyes and how they seemed to stare directly through his as he choked the life out of her had haunted him over the past year. Her body had stopped resisting relatively quickly in an almost complicit manner, but her eyes continued to launch an offensive that he could feel in his soul, even after hers had departed. After looking around to again make sure that nobody had seen the encounter, he quickly tossed her body in the back of his car and sped away.

*Late Life*

The pills, the prostitution, and the pole had already taken Vivian's life away from her long before they had ever even met at Buddy's Speakeasy, he rationalized as he drove along Interstate 90 and tried to come up with a solution for the body strewn across his back seat. While he was certain that nobody would even realize she was missing for at least another day, he wanted to make sure that he disposed of her body as quickly as possible.

Too many people had seen him at Buddy's and that old Chinese woman had even confronted Vivian outside her apartment building late one night as they made their way inside. He knew that even though that old woman, who had yelled at Vivian and called her a whore, might have caught a glimpse of his face, it was very dark outside and he had made sure to turn away as soon as she started berating Vivian.

It didn't matter to him, though. None of that did.

Aside from having a photograph of him, which he knew that they did not possess, he was just going to appear as a middle-aged, overweight, bald white guy in a police artist's sketch.

Even if someone had seen the car he was driving that night and had written down the license plate number, it would only lead them back to whatever car rental company it was stolen from.

It was well-known by the local gangs that all of the car rental companies located at Hopkins International Airport refused to eliminate the practice of leaving the keys in each and every vehicle on the lot in an effort to appease their VIP clientele. To the car rental companies, it was far easier for each of them to deal with a few stolen cars each month that they could write off as a loss than it was to risk losing those priority customers who thoroughly enjoyed being able to check-in and pick any car off the lot that they wanted. God forbid they would have to stand in line with the amateur travelers at the rental counter.

This led to a dozen or so brand new vehicles being driven off the lot every month by enterprising youngsters looking to make some quick cash. All they had to do was hop in the car and carefully drive over the spike strips that really were not much more than a placebo deterrent if they went slowly enough before accelerating, sometimes completely unnoticed, past the workers sitting in the exit booths.

*Late Life*

Airport police had tried, unsuccessfully, to convince the rental companies to rethink their policies because they were tired of trying to track down the stolen cars that sometimes weren't even reported for months after leaving the lot. Once on the streets, the late model vehicles would be sold for as little as a few hundred dollars to anyone willing to fork over the cash. Drug dealers, gang members, and anyone else looking to do something illegal in a car that couldn't be traced back to them were more than happy to do just that.

While he had grown quite fond of the 2008 Dodge Charger that he had bought off of a 17 year old kid not far from where Vivian Tong lived for $1200 a few weeks prior to his first visit to Buddy's, he knew that he'd eventually have to ditch it just like so many had done before him. There would always be more new vehicles to buy for pennies on the dollar, and he knew that he could leave it anywhere in Cleveland with the keys in it, and it would be gone long before the authorities found it.

Even the bogus West Virginia driver's license that he had used to gain admission into Buddy's Speakeasy wouldn't get the authorities anywhere either, because they would be looking for Eugene Lankford - a man they were certain did not exist outside the four corners of that laminated card.

Eugene Lankford did exist though, as his second victim had discovered in a very painful way in October of 2006 when the man who embodied his persona was on vacation in Las Vegas. Ever since then, he had been routinely checking news websites in Southern Utah, waiting for word that his victim's body had finally been found.

It had taken the authorities in Utah much longer to find her body, or what was left of it, than he had anticipated it would. However, Bryce Canyon National Park was a vast place, stretching over 35,000 acres, and he hadn't exactly left her body out in the open either.

Despite its name, Bryce Canyon National Park isn't actually a canyon at all, but rather a collection of sprawling natural amphitheaters along the eastern side of the Paunsaugunt Plateau. While Bryce's distinctive red, orange, and white colored rocks provided spectacular views for visitors, they also made for a convenient place to dispose of a body.

He had long since given up on organized religion, but he was a firm believer in karma. He couldn't help but trust that it had played a huge role in placing him at the same bar as the woman that the authorities had been trying to locate in the weeks leading up to their fateful encounter.

*Late Life*

Sure, she looked a little different than the pictures he had seen all over the news, but within minutes of her saddling up next to him at the Imperial Palace Casino bar in Las Vegas, he knew that it was her.

The woman known as "Deadly Dolly" had picked the wrong lonely looking guy that evening to seduce. Just as he hadn't been looking to kill again, he also hadn't planned on meeting another person who deserved to die as much as she certainly did.

# 10

"Everything alright, Jason?" Coop asked upon seeing Cara's eldest brother, who looked concerned.

Clarence had just dropped the winning pitcher outside the little-known downstairs entrance to MetroHealth Medical Center, just outside the hospital's independent police station, where Jason was waiting for him. Clarence, per protocol, would wait until Coop and Jason were safely inside the hospital before departing.

The chief of Metro's police force, Frank Suchetka, was a retired Cleveland Police officer and one of Clarence's friends from his days on the force. Anytime Coop was at MetroHealth, Frank made sure that at least one armed officer was near the star athlete at all times, but typically there were at least two keeping a watchful eye. Grace Brooks, while off-duty, was also there to support Coop and the officers, if needed.

Having armed officers whenever Coop was inside the hospital not only provided him a sense of added security, but it also enabled Clarence and the staff at CW Security Solutions a much needed break. For Clarence, that meant grabbing some takeout and heading home to see his wife, Evelynn.

"Yeah," Jason replied, unconvincingly, as he gave Coop their usual one-armed 'bro hug'.

"Liar," Coop laughed. "Don't pee on my leg and tell me it's rainin' now…"

"Thank God you said 'liar' before busting out another one of your southern sayings; otherwise, you'd have lost me on that one," Jason answered, hoping to change the subject.

"Plenty more where that came from," Coop chuckled. "But, you're not getting off that easy, Detective…"

"To be honest, it's one of those things that could be nothing," Jason paused for effect. "Or it could be absolutely everything."

"Let me guess," Coop said. "You can't talk about it, either."

"Nail. Head."

"Well, if you ever do need to," Coop began, before Jason interrupted.

"Yeah, yeah, I can come to you. I know…"

"Actually, I was going to say to call Clarence," Coop deadpanned. "He gives *way* better advice than I do…"

The two of them laughed as they walked down the hallway outside the hospitality suite where Cara and the rest of the Knox family had been keeping vigil. Jason had prepped Coop on how each member of the family was doing while in the elevator.

Joanne had been strong, as usual, but lacking the spirit that typically made others stand in awe of her during even the most difficult of times. Perhaps it was the fact that she and Charlie's relationship had been the best it had been since before his accident, and this latest episode was certain to bring back darker times, even in a best case scenario.

Christopher, who was still on his way back from Japan, had phoned Jason during a layover to let him know that he should be back in town within the next day.

Johnny had been quietly dealing with everything, but Jason said that having Grace by his side helped a lot. He even saw Johnny appear to open up to her at one point.

Cara, Jason said, had been wearing her emotions on her sleeve, as usual. It was one of Coop's favorite qualities in his girlfriend. You always knew where you stood with Cara. When Coop pressed Jason more on Cara, her oldest brother admitted that she seemed to really be struggling.

"What about you?" Coop had asked Jason before they exited the elevator. "How are *you* doing?"

"I'm fine. I'm just trying to make sure everyone else is okay," Jason replied dismissively.

"Well, you know if you need to talk to someone," Coop began before Jason tried to beat him to the punch, again.

"Yeah, yeah, I know. Talk to Clarence, right?" Jason laughed.

"No, man. Talk to me!" Coop exclaimed, feigning disappointment, before giving Jason a smirk that could not hide how proud he was to have set the detective up twice with the same bait and switch.

"What does my sister even see in you?" Jason chided, shaking his head.

"You're preaching to the choir, brother…"

"Hey, I almost forgot," Jason said, stopping abruptly just outside the hospitality suite. "Great job on the mound tonight. You were really pumping gas out there!"

"Not gonna lie, it felt good to be back out there in front of the home crowd," Coop replied.

"The best part is," Jason did his best to sound sincere, "All that money I bet on you tonight will make sure little Gabby can have food on the table for another week…"

"Now I know you're lyin'," Coop laughed as the two entered the room.

*Late Life*

# 11

Cara barely seemed to notice Coop as he entered MetroHealth's hospitality suite with Jason. It was late and her eyes were tired and red from all the tears that had been shed over the past two days. Joanne was asleep in the corner chair, her head resting on a U-shaped neck pillow that had been given to her by the hospital chaplain, Marsha Beeching, before she left for the evening.

Johnny and Grace both stood to greet Coop, quietly congratulating him on his pitching performance earlier that evening. Erica, who was holding a sleeping Gabby on her lap, gave a wave and whispered hello.

Cara was the last to stand, clutching one of her father's many cloth handkerchiefs in her hand. Charlie always had a cloth "hanky", as he called them, in his front shirt pocket. He had at least two dozen of them, each of which had been monogrammed with his initials in blue thread by Joanne. Had to be blue, Charlie would insist. That was Ford's color, and despite his accident while working for the automobile giant, he was loyal through and through.

Cara had grabbed this particular one after stopping at her parents' house to get Joanne, who refused to leave the hospital, some fresh clothes. While the handkerchief certainly served a practical purpose for her that evening, just simply holding the familiar cotton cloth in her hand was an added bonus.

Charlie, before his accident, would use his "hankies" to wipe Cara's tears away if she scraped her knee on the playground, lost a tough basketball game, or suffered a heartbreak from a boy. She could still feel his hand dab the incredibly soft cloth on her cheeks as he would insist that everything would be okay.

"Hey, girl," Coop said as he opened his long, muscular arms and pulled her in for an embrace.

"You were awesome tonight," Cara said, keeping her cheek pressed against his broad chest.

Coop didn't reply. Instead he just squeezed her a little tighter and kissed the top of her head.

"You smell good," Cara said, still not moving from his chest. "Different, but good…"

"I'll have to let Higgy know," Coop chuckled, referring to the Tribe's clubhouse attendant, Patrick "Higgy" Higgins. "He put some sort of new body wash stuff in the showers after the guys told him the old stuff was bad luck."

"I loved what you did for the camera after each inning," Cara said, as she finally pulled her face from his chest and looked up. "It was really sweet, and my mom loved it."

"Wish I could do more than make some hand gestures at a TV camera to help…"

"You've done more than that, Coop," she countered. "Do you think the hospital would have given the little old Knox family this hospitality suite if they didn't know you would be here, too?"

"Well, maybe after they saw how pretty you are they would've," Coop tried to use levity to deflect. He knew that his status as a professional athlete provided not only him, but others associated with him, a lot of perks and

access to things that others could only dream of to the point that it made him
feel guilty.

"Do I look pretty now?" Cara asked, pointing to her swollen eyes.

"Gorgeous, actually," Coop answered, immediately.

Cara could almost feel his steely blue eyes penetrate through all of the
pain she had been feeling. It was unfair, at times, Cara thought. Those eyes
had bailed him out of quite a few arguments with her, mostly because once he
locked in on her with them it was as if her feet did not need a floor. His eyes
had the power to remove all of the weight from her soul, and he knew it.

"Hey," Cara began.

"What?"

"Can we just go back to the Wescott?"

"Absolutely," Coop replied, trying not to sound too eager to leave the
hospital for the comforts of his massive penthouse. "As long as you're okay
with leaving, that is…"

"I am. Mom even told me I should go home tonight," Cara said,
nodding towards Joanne. "I wish she would take her own advice…"

"Clarence went home for the night, but I'm sure Grace wouldn't mind taking us there," Coop said.

Jason, overhearing their conversation, chimed in, "I'll take you guys home. I was going to follow Gabby and Erica home anyways."

"Works for me," Coop said.

Cara walked over to where her mom was sitting, kissed her own hand, and then gently placed it on Joanne's head. She wished her mother was sleeping in her own bed as opposed to the lightly padded wooden chair where she lay, but she also knew that she would be doing the same if it was Coop in that recovery room.

There was a time in Cara's life where her father was so miserable that she sometimes thought he would be better off dead. The events of the last year, however, had changed that.

Now, more than ever, she prayed for her father to live.

*Late Life*

# 12

The electronic chirp started as a distant melody at first, but as each note began to enter Cooper Madison's increasingly conscious brain, the melodic tone turned to an annoying intruder trying to steal the final few precious minutes of sleep his body so desperately needed.

Once he finally came to the realization that it was his cell phone, he rolled over and reached across Cara's still slumbering frame and grabbed it from the nightstand. It was his agent, Todd "T-Squared" Taylor.

Coop tried his best to quietly exit the bedroom before answering the call. That was no small task as his body emitted the cracks and pops he had grown accustomed to, especially the morning after he pitched.

"Good morning, T," Coop answered as he walked down the hall of his massive penthouse in the direction of the living room.

"How's my favorite client doing this morning after throwing that gem last night?" Todd asked.

"Wondering why my agent is waking me up this early the day after a start," Coop quipped as he stared at the wall clock above the couch and realized it was barely 7 o'clock in the morning.

"Sorry, brother. I'm in India. Isn't it like noon there?"

"No, it's freaking 7:05, T... Why the hell are you in India?"

"Looking for the next Cooper Madison. You know how many cricket players are in this country? Like a billion, man, and some of them have incredible arms. One of my contacts over here insists that we can turn a few of them into pitchers, so here I am..."

"How's Joy feel about you being halfway across the world while she and the baby are here?" Coop asked with a laugh.

After years of trying, Todd and his wife had finally been blessed with a beautiful daughter last March. Coop had been asked to be the baby's godfather along with Joy's sister, who was the godmother, and they both had used their newfound titles as an excuse to spoil the heck out of her with gifts and love.

72

The baby's name was Alexa Lee Taylor and she had proven to be the first human being ever to make Todd slow down and reduce his travel schedule for work. He absolutely adored his baby daughter, and she him, which is why Coop was surprised that Todd had traveled to India.

"You want me to ask her? She and Alexa are sitting next to me at the hotel restaurant," Todd replied. "Joy has always wanted to see India, and since it's obvious that my daughter is going to be a genius, I figured I'd get her some culture…"

"Only you, T…" Coop laughed.

"How's Cara's dad doing?"

"He's hanging in there. If the creek don't rise, he'll be okay, but it's still very touch and go. He's a tough cookie though."

"And, what about Cara? She doing okay?"

"As expected, I suppose," Coop replied. "You know Cara - she's worried most about her momma and everyone else."

"Understandable," Todd agreed, then changed the subject. "So, how do you feel after throwing last night?"

"Great. I mean, normal soreness, and all. But, I felt good out there."

"That's what I like to hear, brother. Listen, I gotta go - our food is being served now, but I just wanted to check up on you."

"No worries, T. I appreciate it."

"Hey Coop, you want to know something crazy about how they eat here in India?" Todd asked.

"What's that?"

"Every meal is traditionally served way later than we do in the states. Normal breakfast time is at like ten in the morning and dinner isn't until around eight or nine at night."

"That's gotta be rough for an early bird like you. What time is it there now, anyways?"

"4:30 in the afternoon, but my body still thinks it's seven in the morning. We're all screwed up time-wise, especially the baby, but Joy has been a trooper and has kept her on the same feeding schedule. Moms get the short end of the stick when it comes to the parenting thing…"

"Especially when they're married to a globetrotting sports agent," Coop chuckled. "Make sure you buy that woman something nice while you're there."

"You know I already did. I bought matching emerald earrings for both of my girls. Alexa will get to wear hers when I finally let her get her ears pierced. I'm thinking when she's 30 and out of the convent," Todd laughed. "Alright, brother, I'm getting the old 'hang up the phone' look from Joy. She and Alexa both send their love."

"I know that look, too. Be safe and give my goddaughter a big hug for me."

"Will do, Coop, and give my best to Cara and her family. Call with any updates, no matter the time."

After ending the call, Coop made his way back to the bedroom where he found Cara, who was still sound asleep. She was wearing one of his old t-shirts just like she always did, and the oversized garment looked more like a nightgown on her than a shirt.

Coop wished that he could do more to help take the pain away that she was feeling. He was a fixer by nature, but he knew that in situations like these, that wasn't an option. He also understood the pain that accompanied watching a parent suffer, just as he had with his mother when he was a child as she bravely battled cancer.

*Late Life*

He remembered how his late father, Jeffrey, did his best to be strong for his wife, Kelsey, and his son during those extremely difficult months. Coop used to marvel at how his dad would always put on a brave front around him and his mom. But, he also remembered the late nights when he would sometimes hear his father weeping behind a closed bathroom door, unaware that his only son lay still awake down the hall.

Coop wasn't sure if he would be able to be as strong for Cara as his father was for his mom, but he knew that he would do everything in his power to try. He loved that young woman sleeping so peacefully in his bed more than he had ever loved those who came before her, and he would make sure that she never went a day without knowing that to be true.

# 13

Charlie Knox knew that he was dreaming. He had to be. It was the only explanation he could conjure up as he stared down at his legs as they churned forward in a rhythmic cadence on what appeared to be a cinder track.

A ringing bell to his left diverted his eyes away from the fine layer of crushed igneous rock crunching beneath his worn leather track spikes. As he glanced over in the direction of the ringing, he could see Hank Garner, his old track coach at West High, cupping his hands around his mouth as he yelled in his direction.

"Last lap, Knox! Push! Push! Push!"

Charlie could hear the runners approaching behind him. The sound of their spikes grew closer with each stride, but he did not dare to look back.

*Late Life*

That's what Coach Garner had always pounded into his head: Never, ever, look back. Only forward.

His chest burned and each breath he took felt futile as he prayed that more oxygen would reach his overtaxed lungs. Charlie relaxed his shoulders away from his ears, just as he had been coached to do when feeling shortness of breath, but continued to thrust his feet forward as he made his way through the first turn.

He could not see the stands, but he could nonetheless hear the cheers from the crowd grow as he labored down the straightaway, trying his damnedest to distance himself from the approaching pack. He glanced up to see who he would have to catch, hoping that maybe that would give him the motivation to push himself harder, but the long stretch of dark track in front of him was empty.

He was in the *lead*.

It was then that he realized exactly where his dream was taking place.

Charlie had never been a superstar in the mile. He had always finished in the middle of the pack, sometimes even in the rear. That is, however, until his very last race as a senior at the conference championship when he ran the race of his life.

Well, what could have been the race of his life, he thought.

Charlie had been in the lead heading into the last 100 meters when the moment became too much for him. He had never been all alone in the front of a race, and as he tried desperately to fend off the fastly approaching pack, his chest tightened up so much that he could not breathe.

He tried to battle through it and tears streamed down his face as he willed his body to do what it had never done before. However, with 10 meters to go, the conference favorite, Danny Mirtich from John Marshall, sped past him and claimed the title.

Charlie, who should have been happy with his runner-up finish based off of his mediocre high school track career, was devastated. He had blown his one chance to be anything more than average in a life that he was certain would be anything but mundane as an adult. He wasn't going to go to college, and he would likely be drafted into the service after graduation, just as all the other working class guys he knew had been.

*Late Life*

As his legs continued to churn, Charlie realized that he was getting another chance to win the race that had haunted him his entire life.

"Last hundred, Knox!" Coach Garner bellowed. "Push!"

Charlie could feel a solitary runner gaining on him as he thrust himself forward. It was Mirtich. It had to be. He was 20 meters from the finish line now, determined to fend off his opponent, whose steps were growing closer with each stride.

*Not this time…*

Charlie ran with everything he had those last 20 meters, his eyes locked in on the rope that stretched across the finish line. He was not going to lose his second chance at greatness.

Charlie hurled his body at the rope and felt the nylon braids slide down his torso as he stumbled to the ground, unable to breathe. No matter how much he opened his mouth, the oxygen evaded his lungs.

He could see Coach Garner's worn Florsheim Shoes on the ground next to him as he struggled to breathe. Charlie tried to look up at his coach. Perhaps he could communicate with his eyes that he desperately needed air, only Hank Garner was no longer there.

Instead, he saw his wife, Joanne. She was clasping his right hand in hers, her left clasped over top, with tears in her eyes.

"It's okay, Charlie," she whispered as she lifted his hand in hers and softly pressed them against her cheek.

He wanted to tell her that he had won the race, knowing that she would be so proud, but every attempt was futile.

"It's okay, Charlie," Joanne repeated.

With those words, Charlie no longer felt like he couldn't breathe. In fact, he felt a strong sense of serenity as he stared into his wife's eyes.

"I love you, Charlie Knox," Joanne whispered, as tears streamed down her cheeks.

Charlie hoped that his eyes would tell her everything he was feeling in that moment. That he loved her more than life itself. That she was the best mother to their four beautiful children. That she was the strongest woman he knew and that he was thankful that she stood by him after the accident that had left him paralyzed, even when he did his best to drive her away in his darkest of days.

"It's okay, Charlie," she whispered. "It's okay. I love you so much, Charlie."

Maybe she had understood what his eyes were trying to say, he thought. Regardless, he felt that she knew, and that was all that mattered.

Charlie Knox tried to keep his eyes open. He wanted to stare into Joanne's eyes forever.

"It's okay, Charlie…"

Joanne's voice sounded as if it was fading.

"I love you, Charlie Knox…"

When he opened his eyes again, Charlie found himself standing atop the old wooden podium facing the stadium bleachers at West High School. He looked down at the 1st place medal that hung around his neck and then back up at the cheering spectators.

In the front row was Joanne, who was standing and smiling as she clapped. Next to her were their children and their families, who were also applauding. Familiar faces of relatives and friends filled the grandstand. He saw his aunts, Connie and Kim, his sister, Anne, and his uncle, Bobby. All of them were smiling, cheering, and clapping for Charlie, who raised his hands

victoriously in the air towards the bright light of the sun.

*Late Life*

# 14

Jason Knox had just sat down at his office desk inside Cleveland Police's 1st District headquarters when his phone rang. He put down his favorite coffee mug, which his daughter, Gabby, had painted him for Father's Day that year, and answered the call.

"This is Detective Knox," Jason said into the receiver.

"Detective Knox, this is United States Marshal Brad Coreno. I'm out here in southern Utah and have been assigned a case involving a Jane Doe who was apparently stabbed to death and found in Bryce Canyon National Park. The local authorities here said that you had called them yesterday and that you might have a lead on what we're dealing with here," the man with a gravely voice on the other end of the line stated. His cadence indicated that he was likely former military.

Jason had been expecting the call. After speaking with Hannah LaMarca, he had phoned Bryce Canyon's U.S. Park Police office and requested to speak to whomever was in charge of the investigation.

"I'm glad you called, Marshal Coreno," Jason replied.

"Please, call me Brad. I'm not that fancy of a guy."

"Fair enough, as long as you call me Jason. Listen, the reason I called is because I think I might know who the Jane Doe is, or at least the name she went by..."

"I'm listening," Brad said.

"I'm not sure if you've ever heard of a case we worked here in Cleveland called the EPK, or Edgewater Park Killer, but there's a chance that the two cases could be related."

"I'm familiar with it. I saw the Dateline episode. You guys did a great job with that case," Brad answered.

"Depends who you ask," Jason chuckled.

"Trust me, I understand. So, why do you think our Jane Doe is possibly related to your EPK case?"

Jason knew that whatever answer that Brad gave to his next question would determine whether or not he had just wasted the Marshal's time. Part of Jason wanted that to be the case. He would simply apologize and move on with his life. On the other hand, if Brad confirmed it to be true, Jason realized that his life was about to get far more complicated.

"I'm not sure what you're at liberty to divulge about the case at this point, Brad, but I have a question about the knife found at the scene."

"The buck knife?" Brad replied. "What about it?"

Jason swallowed hard before asking, "Did it happen to have anything inscribed on the handle?"

"It did," Brad confirmed, without adding anything else to his reply. He was not about to tip his hand to a detective he had never met, and Jason knew that he would have to provide more if the veteran Marshal was going to divulge anything further.

"I have a source, someone I trust very much," Jason began, referring to Hannah. "She said that the knife looked as if it was a souvenir, the kind that tourist traps sell, and that it had 'Gatlinburg' inscribed on the handle. Is that true?"

"I'd say that you have a very reliable source," Brad answered. "To be honest, Jason, I was hoping that's why you were calling because if I recall correctly from the Dateline episode, that's where the infamous Dolly was last seen. Full disclosure, I was going to call both you and the Gatlinburg PD this morning to follow up on it. Even though it could very well be circumstantial at best, the victim's remains are likely that of a middle-aged woman."

"What's your gut telling you, Brad?" Jason asked. "I mean, the odds have to be slim to none that it's Dolly, right?"

"One thing I've learned doing this job is that every now and then we are reminded that the world is a much smaller place than we think it is. While it's a bit of a stretch, I know that I'm hoping this is one of those situations."

"What can I do on my end to help?"

"Well, I can tell you that I have at least a few days of phone calls ahead of me trying to see if I can nail down where this knife might have been purchased in Gatlinburg and whether or not there's a chance that we could get any sort of confirmation that someone matching Dolly's description purchased it. In the meantime it's imperative that this information doesn't get out any further than it already has. The last thing we need right now is the media

trying to solve this case on conjecture," Brad replied.

"I'll talk to my source and make sure it stays that way on her end,"

Jason offered even though Brad hadn't actually asked him to. He knew that

Hannah would likely have to report on the story which was certain to start

making the rounds on broadcasts all over the country, but he also knew that

she would do so in a way that did not include any of the details that Brad

Coreno wanted to keep under wraps.

"Good. In the meantime just wait to hear back from me. As soon as I

know something on my end, I'll be in touch."

"Good deal," Jason replied.

"Oh, and one more thing…"

"What's that?"

"Give my best to Miss LaMarca…"

The call ended before a dumbfounded Jason could even try and refute

the fact that Hannah was his source.

As Jason replayed the entire conversation with Brad in his head, trying

to figure out if he had accidentally said her name, there was one thing he knew for sure. Brad Coreno was obviously a smart guy and someone that Jason was really looking forward to working with wherever the case took them.

# 15

"Do you know that I've been sitting across the bar for over an hour waiting for you to come over and buy me a drink?"

The man known as Eugene Lankford grinned as he recalled the fateful night that past October inside the lounge at Las Vegas's Imperial Palace. The news of the body discovered in Bryce Canyon National Park had just been featured during Hannah LaMarca's evening broadcast on Channel One.

The 24 hour news cycle had created a need for local news stations to report on stories from across the globe far more than they did in the days of two evening broadcasts, so it was no surprise to him that the story had been picked up so quickly by Cleveland's most watched news network. There just wasn't enough local news to fill five broadcasts an evening.

*Late Life*

The man never missed Hannah's broadcasts and like most men in Cleveland, he had a bit of a crush on her. Hearing her recount the grizzly discovery and knowing that she was really talking about his crime only made his attraction to her grow stronger.

That evening back in Vegas he had, in fact, noticed her the moment he sat down at the bar. However, he must have missed whatever signals she thought that she was giving him.

The woman, who appeared to be in her early 50's, displayed a curvy physique that had been packed into a pair of tight jeans and blouse that didn't leave much to the imagination. Her frizzy hair was jet black, obviously the result of a dye job that looked anything but professional, and she made sure to gently press her ample chest into his shoulder as she leaned in to talk over the loud music that was playing.

"I'm sorry," he had replied, making no effort to move his shoulder away from her left breast as she leaned in even closer.

"So, are you here alone in Sin City?" she purred into his ear.

It had been a long time since he had been pursued by a woman. Sure, after his messy divorce he had a couple flings, but those were all with strippers and prostitutes like Vivian Tong.

While she was far from the type of woman he would normally be attracted to, the fact that she was pursuing him immediately made her seem more attractive by the second. It also didn't hurt that he was on day two of a bender, far from sober, and she had just placed her hand on his thigh.

"Yup, flying solo," he answered as he leaned in close enough to smell her cheap perfume. "What about you?"

"Single and ready to mingle," she confirmed, making sure to gently brush her lips against his ear as she spoke.

"Well, then. How about I buy you that drink?"

"Only if you promise to let me thank you for it later," she cooed.

"I'm sure we could work something out," he said with a wink before gesturing to the bartender, who then came over to take their order.

"I'll take whatever he's having," she said.

"Two more vodka and cranberries, please," he ordered, placing a twenty on the bar. "Keep the change."

"Look at you, big spender," she said as she squeezed his thigh.

"I don't know about that, but I have had a *very* good day at the blackjack tables..."

"Are you still feeling lucky?" she whispered in his ear, her hand moving further up his thigh.

"Like the dealer just dealt me a pair of aces to split and he's showing a seven," he laughed.

"Is that good?" she asked, batting her eyes. "I don't know anything about blackjack…"

"Yes, that's very good, but I'm kind of done playing cards for the night. I have some other games I'd rather play."

The bartender returned with the drinks before she could answer. She picked hers up and raised the rock glass in a toast.

"Here's to showing me just what it is you have in mind for after we finish these drinks," she declared.

"I'll drink to that," he said, raising his glass in return. "What's your name, anyways, gorgeous?"

"Rebecca," she replied after taking a long sip.

"That's a beautiful name for a beautiful woman."

"Well, aren't you just the sweetest. My daddy named me after his favorite singer," she said.

"Hmmm. You got me on that one. I can't think of a famous singer named Rebecca," he replied, sipping his drink.

"Well, Rebecca was her middle name, actually. You'd probably know her better as Dolly Parton."

It took a second before her words registered in his alcohol fogged brain, but then it hit him like a Nolan Ryan fastball.

"Are you okay, sweetie?" she asked when he failed to respond.

Collecting himself, and doing his best not to show the excitement that was building inside his body, he replied with a smile, "Oh, yes, sorry. It's just that I, too, am a big Dolly Parton fan."

"Well then, I guess it's karma that we met."

"I couldn't have said it any better myself," he said, raising his glass again.

"So, are you going to tell me your name, too? Or should I just call you Sexy Mr. Clean?" she laughed, playfully rubbing the top of his bald head.

*Late Life*

"How rude of me," he said staring into her eyes. "It's Eugene. Eugene Lankford."

# 16

Cara stood behind her mother as she watched her father take his last breath. Two days had passed since Charlie's team of doctors had tried, unsuccessfully, to revive him after the therapeutic hypothermia treatment.

After Charlie's body had been re-warmed over an 8 hour period to his normal body temperature, the doctors determined that the chances of Charlie coming out of the coma on his own would be very slim.

"We can continue to intubate Mr. Knox in hopes that he will emerge from the coma," Dr. Kathryn Dye had informed the family shortly after the re-warming procedure had concluded.

"What if he doesn't?" Jason had asked.

"We can continue to keep him intubated and hope for the best, but ultimately that will be up to you, Joanne," Dr. Dye replied, nodding towards

Joanne. "Since you have the medical power of attorney, it's really up to you how long you want to keep Charlie intubated."

"So, basically you're just keeping him alive right now?" Johnny chimed in.

"The ventilator is definitely keeping Charlie stable," she answered.

"How long?" Joanne, who had been silent throughout the entire conversation, asked. "How long will he have if we choose to remove the breathing tube?"

"It's hard to say," Dr. Dye replied. "It really depends on the level of brain function that Mr. Knox may or may not still have. Patients with zero brain function tend to go within minutes after removing the breathing tube, because they won't be able to breathe on their own. Charlie's scans show some small activity, though, and in other cases like this that I've seen before, the patient can survive for hours or even days."

"Is there any chance he could still make a recovery?" Jason asked.

"While I have seen some miraculous things happen, and I'm not saying it won't happen in Charlie's case, but I also don't want to give any of you false hope," Dr. Dye replied. "My hope for Charlie is that we will continue to give him all the meds we can to ensure that he is as comfortable as possible after removing the support. Assuming his brain function scans were accurate, he will be able to breathe on his own. He may even be able to open his eyes, but don't be surprised if he doesn't."

"Will he be able to hear us?" Cara asked.

"While we won't have any way of knowing for sure, there is a possibility. I've had patients in similar situations open their eyes occasionally and even squeeze the hands of a family member in response to questions," Dr. Dye responded. "Here's what I do know for sure. We will do everything in our power to make him as comfortable as possible, and you will all be able to comfort him and be by his side for as long as his body will allow him to breathe."

Joanne took a few steps toward Dr. Dye and placed her hands on the physician's before asking, "If this was your husband, what would you do?"

Dr. Dye gave Joanne a sincere smile and said, "I know that my husband would not want to be kept alive by a machine, and I also know that he would want to have his family around him whether he could hear their words, or not. That being said, only you know best what Charlie would want. I'm going to give you all some time as a family to discuss what you would like us to do. Marsha will also be here to help in any way that she can."

After Dr. Dye left the room, Marsha Beeching, the hospital chaplain, invited the family to sit down on the couches in the hospitality suite. It didn't take long for the family to reach a decision, as hard as it was.

When Marsha brought Dr. Dye back into the suite, Joanne informed her that the family had decided to remove Charlie from life support, but not until after Christopher arrived from Japan.

The next morning, after a tired and weary Christopher had made it to the hospital, Charlie was removed from life support. He was able to breath on his own, but Dr. Dye informed the family that she didn't think he would make it more than a day or two based off of his lung function.

That first day, Joanne and each of Charlie's four children spent time alone with their father, holding his hand and saying all of the things that they wanted to say. Some of Charlie's closest friends, including his Ford Plant buddies, Stucky and Ed Delaney, were also able to say their goodbyes. Even Coop spent some time alone with Charlie, where he tearfully promised him that he would always look after his only daughter for him.

Charlie managed to keep fighting for almost 36 hours, but when his breathing became noticeably more labored, the doctors notified the family that it would not be long before his body finally shut down.

Coop swore that he saw Charlie's eyes open briefly just prior to taking his final breath as Joanne held his hand and comforted him, telling him that everything was okay and that she loved him. He had joined the Knox family in Charlie's room and did his best to be strong for all of them while they all tearfully saw Charlie through to the end.

Once Dr. Dye confirmed Charlie's passing, the Knox children gathered around their mother in a tearful embrace. Despite knowing for the past two days that Charlie's passing was inevitable, everyone in the room held on to a small hope that he would be the exception.

Coop felt a gentle hand on his shoulder and turned to see Chaplain Marsha Beeching's comforting eyes.

"Thank you for being here," Coop whispered as he gave her a hug. "This was so hard…"

"I know it was," she whispered back, maintaining the embrace. "Just remember, young man, that there will be more hard times ahead. Cara is going to go through a lot of emotions, especially over the next few weeks."

"You have any advice for me?" he asked.

"I do," she said, gesturing for him to follow her to the hallway outside Charlie's room.

The veteran chaplain stared Coop in the eyes and advised, "Let her feel all the emotions and even if she seems like she wants you to fix it, remember that you can't. All you can do is be there for her and give her the safety to grieve. Don't be surprised if she gets angry at you over little things or even starts an irrational argument. It's natural for someone in Cara's position to test the people they love the most after the loss of a loved one, but I have a feeling you'll pass any test she may conjure up."

"I'll do my best," Coop said.

"That's all you can do, young man."

# 17

Hannah LaMarca stood on the steps outside of the Cleveland Police Department's 1st Precinct holding two cups of coffee, waiting for Detective Jason Knox to meet her.

Today was his first day back on the job since his father's funeral one week earlier. Jason had opted to use some of the personal leave time that he had accrued to help with the funeral arrangements and assist his mother in taking care of all of the tasks that accompany the passing of a spouse. Finalizing financial documents, enacting insurance policies, and even moving Charlie's hospital bed out of her house had more than kept him busy during that time.

*Late Life*

Hannah had attended the funeral. It was a somber, yet beautiful occasion. Not only were Charlie's family and friends in attendance, but also every single one of Coop's baseball teammates and coaches.

Due to the massive turnout, the service was conducted at Cleveland's Old Stone Church. Ed Delaney, Charlie's best friend and godfather to Cara, used his connections as president of the UAW 1250 to secure the historic place of worship.

Old Stone Church, founded in 1820 when Cleveland was no more than a village with a few hundred residents, had seating for over 600 people inside its downtown location. To anyone walking past the venerable house of worship, shadowed on all sides by some of Cleveland's largest buildings, it was a reminder of just how much the city had grown since it was first erected.

It was at the funeral that Jason had pulled Hannah aside and asked her to meet him at the precinct once he returned to work. Since it wasn't the time or place for her to ask about specifics, she just agreed and promised to meet him at 8 o'clock sharp on that Monday.

"Please tell me one of those is for me," Jason said as he approached Hannah. "I am dragging ass today."

"I figured as much," Hannah said as she handed him a cup.

"You're a saint," he said as he raised his cup in a toast.

"How are you holding up?"

"Hangin' in there, I suppose. Erica has been great, but Gabby has been taking it pretty hard. Erica never knew her dad, so Charlie was the only grandpa Gabby had."

"Oh, that poor thing," Hannah replied. "What about Joanne? How is she doing?

"Well, she's keeping busy. Aside from the funeral, I'm not really sure I've seen her grieve. I think she's doing her best to put on a strong front for everyone. You know something? I think she has given up so much of who she is while taking care of my dad ever since the accident, that I'm not really sure she knows how to do anything else."

"That's understandable," Hannah agreed.

"I know that she has probably imagined, hell, even prayed for what life would be like when she didn't have to take care of Dad. Now that it's here, I'm not sure she's ready for it."

"It'll take time, I'm sure. How's everyone else?" Hannah asked as they began to take a walk.

"Well, Christopher flew back to Japan the day after the funeral. He claimed that he had to, but I know he doesn't do well with stuff like this. He's the most like my dad, personality wise, so staying here and dealing with the sadness just wasn't in the cards. My dad would've done the same thing," Jason chuckled.

"How about Johnny?"

"Johnny's the most emotional one out of all of us kids, so he's been struggling. But, he's lucky to have Grace. She's good for him and I know he'll be okay."

"And Cara? She seemed to be taking it the hardest at the funeral."

"As expected. She was 'Daddy's Little Girl', you know. Coop said that she was a mess the first few days after Dad passed, and even more so after the funeral. She's been helping Mom out though. I'm just worried how she'll do after Coop leaves tonight for his team's road trip. He's going to be gone for the next week on the west coast."

"He seems like a really good guy, which in my experience with professional athletes is a rarity," Hannah said with a laugh.

"He is a really good dude," Jason agreed.

The pair walked in silence for a minute before Hannah asked, "So, why'd you want to meet with me today? I'm assuming it has something to do with the body they found in Utah?"

"It does," Jason confirmed. "And I appreciate you standing down like I asked you to in regards to releasing any details about the possible connections to our case."

"No need to thank me. I totally understand why that U.S. Marshal guy wanted you to tell me to lay off. What was his name again?"

"Nice try, Miss LaMarca," Jason laughed. "You and I both know I never told you what his name was…"

"Hey, it was worth a shot," Hannah conceded.

"What I can tell you, and this is the reason I asked you here today, is that we may have a lead on where the knife that was found at the scene was purchased."

"Go on…" Hannah encouraged, trying hard not to show just how excited she was.

"According to my contact with the Marshal service, the knife did, in fact, have 'Gatlinburg' inscribed on the handle."

"Ha! I knew it!" Hannah interrupted, almost shouting with joy and glad to know that her own source out in Utah was a trustworthy one.

Jason let her have her moment before adding, "What's better yet is the fact that exact knife is only made and sold at one shop in Gatlinburg. Better yet, it's a one-of-a-kind knife. Only one in existence. It's from a little place called Smokey Mountain Cutlery, and you know what else?"

"Don't tell me - they have a record of who purchased the knife?" Hannah asked, wishing it to be true.

"Better yet," Jason replied. "They have store surveillance footage of a woman fitting Dolly's description purchasing said knife during the time that we know she and Phil Worthington were in Gatlinburg."

"Holy. Shit."

"Exactly," Jason agreed. "This is huge."

"So, what's next? I mean, it's obvious that the body is Dolly, right?"

"It certainly would seem likely, but there's only one problem."

"What?" Hannah pressed.

"We don't know Dolly's real identity, so there's no way of confirming it's her. Whoever she really is…"

"Do they have any leads as to what her real name is? I mean, can't they use dental records or something?" Hannah asked.

"You watch too many movies," Jason chuckled. "Could they? Possibly, but only if they had a list of records to compare hers to."

"Wait," Hannah said. "What about DNA? They already made a connection between her DNA at the other two crime scenes. Can't they test this body and see if it's a match?"

"Yes," Jason replied. "And, they already are in the process of running those tests, but it can take weeks or even months for those results to come back."

"So, what happens in the meantime?"

"As far as you and I are concerned, nothing," Jason said. "I just wanted you to know that you were right and that at some point, hopefully soon, we will have some more answers. The Marshal service is focusing their time and resources on how the body ended up in Bryce Canyon National Park. My contact said that, as of now, they are flying blind and waiting to catch a break that will lead them in the right direction."

"You know that this is killing me to sit on a story this big, right?" Hannah laughed.

"I know, I know," Jason relented. "That being said, I really trust my contact with the Marshal service. I think he's pretty damn smart. However, I also told him that if the case goes cold, that I'm not going to stop you from running a story with what little we do have, because maybe that will produce more leads."

"Fair enough, Detective," Hannah said. "I'll hold you to it."

"Hey, have you asked Scriv to look into this at all?" Jason asked, referring to Cliff Scriven, the former detective turned private investigator that had played an invaluable role during the EPK case.

"I'd love to," Hannah replied, "but he's in the middle of a 21 day cruise through the Mediterranean."

"Must be nice!" Jason laughed.

"Tell me about it!" Hannah agreed. "He had told me that he promised his wife that he would take her on that trip years ago. He said that after working the EPK case that it was time for him to follow through on his pledge. It's going to kill him to find out that he's missing out on this…"

"Once a detective, always a detective," Jason sighed.

"I figured that you could relate," Hannah said with a smile.

"Speaking of," Jason began, "I better get back inside."

"Sounds good," Hannah replied. "I'll be waiting to hear from you."

Jason grinned as he began to walk away and mused, "I know you will, Miss LaMarca."

*Late Life*

# 18

Joanne Knox sat at her kitchen table going through an old photo album. It was the first time she had spent the day alone since the passing of her husband, Charlie. As much as she had appreciated having family and friends staying at her house and helping her, she found herself enjoying the solitude as she flipped through the pages of memories.

She smiled when she came across a photograph of Charlie and her standing together in front of one of their favorite restaurants, the Cabin Club in Westlake. The picture, taken on their anniversary, was the last one she had of the two of them prior to Charlie's accident at the Ford Plant that left him confined to a wheelchair.

*Late Life*

Just like many adults, Joanne had always categorized her marriage based on milestones and other major life changes. She would often say things like, "Before we had kids" when prefacing a story.

This picture represented the last time their life was known as, "Before the accident". The years that followed were terribly hard, not only on Charlie, but also on Joanne.

She found herself in the role of caregiver, as opposed to that of a wife and lover. Over time, Joanne and Charlie's relationship had deteriorated so much that she often fantasized of a life without him.

Things had changed, for the better, over the last year though. She and her husband had finally started to find happiness in their marriage. They would go on a date at least once a week, express their feelings for each other, and Joanne had even started sleeping in the same bedroom as Charlie for the first time since his accident.

Now, in the cruelest of ways, life had taken that all away from her. Joanne wondered what she had done to deserve this kind of misfortune in her life. While she didn't take all of the other blessings that life had given her for granted, like her children, she certainly felt as though she and Charlie had been given a raw deal, nonetheless.

She felt the anger build inside her, and the image of she and Charlie standing in front of the restaurant began to blur through the tears of rage that were welling up in her eyes.

With clenched fists, she raised her arms high above her head and screamed as she began to pound the table over and over.

Ten seconds later, Joanne stared at her trembling hands. She felt stupid for the painful outburst, certain that her hands would start to swell up soon, but she also felt a sense of relief. Joanne had done her best to hold it together since Charlie's death, wanting to show her family and friends that she was strong, but it was all a facade. She felt as fragile as she ever had in her life.

Slowly, she closed the album, unsure what the future had in store for her next, and wept.

*Late Life*

# 19

"Are you sure you're gonna be okay while I'm gone?" Coop asked Cara as he zipped up his suitcase.

He and his teammates were scheduled to depart Hopkins International Airport in less than two hours for a six night, six game west coast road trip. It would be the first time since Charlie's passing that Coop and Cara would be apart, and he was worried how his absence would affect her already fragile state of mind.

"I told you, I'll be fine," Cara replied, trying to hide the fact that she knew that she would be anything but.

"I'm gonna miss you, girl," he said as he wrapped his strong arms around her.

Cara looked up at him, her eyes still puffy from just an hour earlier when she had cried alone in the shower. She didn't want Coop to know that his impending departure was tearing her up inside, but she also knew that he could see through her facade.

"I'm going to miss you, too," she replied, placing her cheek against his broad chest. She could feel the tears coming back again.

"Are you sure you don't want to ride with me to the airport?" he asked. "Clarence will bring you back if you want to go."

Cara wanted to go with him, but she knew that would make this goodbye even harder on both of them. She felt guilty that he was so worried about her, and while it did provide some comfort to know that he cared so much, she also knew that he was scheduled to pitch the next night and needed to be in the right frame of mind to perform.

"I'm positive," she answered.

"I'll call you as soon as we land," he said, kissing her on the top of her head as he squeezed her tightly.

"You better," she countered.

"Remember, Clarence said to call him at any time, regardless of the hour, if you need anything," Coop reminded her, just as he had about a dozen times throughout the day.

"I know…"

"Well, I better get going. Clarence is waiting for me downstairs."

Cara pulled her head away from his chest and looked up into his steely eyes, doing her best to keep it together until he was out the door.

"I love you," she said.

Coop smiled and kissed her softly on the lips.

"I love you more," he replied.

"Nothing…" she whispered, her voice cracking a bit.

"Nothing…" he replied before pulling her tight one last time.

A few minutes later, a tearful Cara watched from the balcony as Coop climbed into the back of Clarence's SUV. She began to sob uncontrollably as the shiny black Escalade pulled away from the Westcott, finally able to let go of all the emotions she had been bottling up for the past day.

Cara knew that she would be okay while he was gone, but the finality of his departure betrayed that confidence. She sat down on one of the balcony's plush outdoor chairs, buried her face into the sleeves of the sweatshirt Coop had been wearing earlier that day, and wept.

She had pulled the sweatshirt out of the hamper immediately after Coop left the penthouse that they shared, and put it on. Cara found comfort in the cotton blend garment, which still bore traces of Coop's musk.

Cara knew that Coop would call her every chance he got while away, and while she loved that about him, she found herself dreading those calls at the same time. Each phone call would have to be accompanied by a goodbye, and those were always the hardest.

Sure, she would have plenty of things to do to keep her busy during his absence. Her best friend, Lucy Eckert, had promised to come over to the Wescott the next night to watch Coop pitch on TV and spend the night afterwards. Cara was also going to spend most of the days at her mom's house, helping her in any way that she could, and later that week she had planned to take Gabby to the zoo.

However, as Cara looked out from the balcony towards the sun that was setting over Lake Erie, she wasn't sure that she would be as strong as she had promised Coop that she would be while he was away.

# 20

Mick McCarthy looked out his office window at Cleveland's 1st Precinct. His longtime partner, Jason Knox, was heading up the steps that lead back inside the building. Mick had watched as Jason and Channel One's Hannah LaMarca said their goodbyes after a long walk together.

Mick knew that Jason and Hannah were close, going back to the early days of the EPK case, and he never really liked the fact that Knox had put so much trust in a member of the media. While he had hoped that today's meeting was just a casual one, he also knew that it probably had something to do with the "Deadly Dolly" case.

Jason had filled Mick in on everything right after Hannah had first called regarding the body found in Bryce Canyon National Park, and again after he spoke with Brad Coreno of the U.S. Marshal Service. Knox had even told him about the security camera footage from the knife shop in Gatlinburg.

"So, what's new with the lovely Hannah LaMarca?" Mick asked Jason, who had just taken a seat across from his commander.

Jason had assumed that Hannah's visit to the precinct would spread like wildfire. A police station was no different than any other office setting when it came to gossip, so when a local celebrity is spotted on the steps outside the building it makes for good fodder.

"Word travels fast," Jason said with a chuckle.

"That's for sure," Mick agreed. "But, I actually saw you. I happened to be at my window when my 'Hot Chick' radar went off."

"I wish your 'Bad Guy' radar worked as well as that one does," Jason teased.

"Insubordination will not be tolerated in this precinct, Knox," Mick mockingly chastised his subordinate.

"They say attitude reflects leadership, Mick…"

"Yeah, yeah…" Mick sighed. "So, what was that all about, anyways? Please tell me that she was hoping you'd set me up with her…"

"For starters, I don't think she's a 'Chubby Chaser'," Jason laughed. "And second, I was just filling her in on where we stand with that body out in Utah. Told her to continue to hold off on any stories she might want to air on it possibly linking the body to Dolly."

"You know I don't like the fact she is getting any info from us, Knox. I don't trust the media," Mick said, his tone serious for a change. "They're all snakes, especially the pretty ones with long legs…"

"I know," Jason relented. "But, without her tip, we wouldn't have even known about the body to begin with. It's only right that I keep her in the loop. Besides, it's not even a CPD case. So… No harm, no foul."

"I'll make sure to make you eat that last part when she throws us under the bus on TV," Mick warned, only half kidding.

"Fair enough," Jason said. "But, I still don't know why you're worried about that. Even if the Jane Doe is Dolly, she never committed a crime in Cleveland. I'm not sure how anyone could possibly place any blame on us."

"Sometimes, Knox, I think you're the dumbest 'smart' guy I know," Mick sighed, shaking his head. "They'll always find a way to point the blame on regular cops like you and me. They'll say we should've caught Phil

123

Worthington before he ever went down to Tennessee, and that if we would've,
then none of this shit would even matter."

"She wouldn't do that, Mick…"

"I admire your faith in her, Knox, but just be careful. The more that
piece of eye candy knows, the more she can use against us later…"

Jason's cell phone chirped to life before Mick could pile on his words
of wisdom any further. Seeing that the call was coming from Cara, he excused
himself from Mick's office and into the hallway.

"What's up, Carebear?"

"Nothing," she replied. "Just wanted to see how your first day back on
the job was going."

Jason could tell that his baby sister had been crying, but she was
trying to hide it. He also knew his baby sister well enough to know that he
shouldn't bring it up.

"Oh, it's going, I suppose. I got in around six this morning and had a
mountain of paperwork and emails waiting for me. You know, real cool
detective stuff," he mused.

That actually got a laugh out of Cara, who quipped, "Oh yeah, I think I saw the same thing on an episode of 'Law and Order' last week…"

"What do you have planned for today?" Jason asked.

"Nothing much. I'll probably get some food from Stucky's later and watch 'The Notebook' for like the tenth time. You know, real self-pity type stuff…"

"That's the chick flick with the guy from 'Remember the Titans', right?" Jason asked.

"Um, you mean Ryan Gosling?" Cara asked, incredulously.

"You'd know better than me," Jason laughed. "I only know him as the guy that was an absolute liability on defense."

"Yeah, well, he's gorgeous and I don't care if he was the worst fictional football player that ever put on a uniform," Cara asserted.

"That's the difference between you and me, I guess," Jason chuckled. "I need to know that my leading man can handle himself in man-to-man coverage and not just look good in a uniform."

"You're such a dork…"

"Hey, you called me, remember?"

"Yeah, but that doesn't change the fact that you're a dork…"

"Fair enough," Jason relented. "But, in all seriousness, if you need anything while Coop's gone, just call me, okay?"

"I will," Cara promised.

"You better, kiddo."

"I'll let you get back to that important police work," Cara said. "I hear there's a lot of emails that are threatening the safety of the city. Better get on that, Detective."

"Fighting crime, one mouse-click at a time, is my new slogan…"

"Hey Jason," Cara said, her tone serious. "I love you…"

"Love you, too, Carebear…"

# 21

"You think Cara's going to be okay while you're out of town?" Clarence asked his most important client, who was seated in the back of his luxury SUV as it pulled away from the Westcott.

"She's doing her best to hide her feelings," Coop replied. "You know how she is."

"I figured as much," Clarence agreed.

"I feel awful, though…"

"I understand," Clarence said. "But, this had to happen sooner or later. It's going to be tough on both of you, but in the end it will make your relationship stronger."

"Man, I sure hope so," Coop sighed as he looked out the window.

"Did I ever tell you about the time that I didn't see Evelynn for almost a month?" Clarence asked, referring to his wife.

"No sir," Coop answered. "I can't imagine that Miz Walters was real happy about that."

"You could say that," Clarence laughed.

"When was this?"

"Well, it was during our first year of marriage," Clarence replied.

"Oh boy, now I got to know the story!"

"You see, I had always wanted to work in the VICE unit. You know, going undercover and penetrating the gangs. All that cool stuff you see in the movies. Well, about six months into our marriage I finally got the call to join the narcotics task force and do just that."

"No way! You got to go undercover?"

"Deep undercover," Clarence chuckled. "So deep that I wasn't allowed to have any contact with my wife or anyone inside the department for what was supposed to be a week long operation. Only that week turned into two, then three, and eventually an entire month."

"How'd she know that you were okay?" Coop asked.

"The department had a liaison who would check in with Evelynn about once a week, just to let her know that I was okay and that I was going to be gone for longer than anticipated."

"I bet that was hard on her."

"It was hard on both of us," Clarence countered. "Meanwhile, I had to become one of the scumbags that I was normally trying to bust…"

"What was your cover?" Coop asked. "That's what it's called, right?"

"The department actually handled coming up with my fake identity, complete with a backstory that I had to memorize so much to the point that by the end of the operation I truly felt like I had become that person."

"What was your fake identity? Or are you not allowed to say?"

"Luther Briggs," Clarence replied. "But my street name was 'Zeus'…"

"Zeus?" Coop laughed. "That's pretty badass, Clarence. You could definitely pass for a 'Zeus'…"

"Yessir," Clarence agreed. "And, I did, man. I became 'Zeus' in every way, shape, and form. My backstory was that I had just arrived from Chicago, where I was wanted for trafficking crack cocaine. The department even went as far as creating a false criminal record, just in case someone within the gang had connections inside the department to do a background check. I had a fake ID, an unregistered gun, and about 10 G's in cash we had confiscated. They set me up in a crappy motel in the neighborhood that the gang controlled, dropped me off, and then I was on my own."

"That's crazy! Were you scared?"

"Hell yeah, I was scared!" Clarence laughed. "This gang I was trying to break in with was no joke, Coop. They were ruthless, man. If they ever found out I was an undercover cop they wouldn't have thought twice about putting a round in my head and dumping my body in front of city hall."

"How long did it take you to get in with the gang?" Coop pressed, visibly excited to learn more.

"Well, the first few days I was there I pretty much laid low and observed. I watched who was working the corners and how the exchanges went down. I had orders to make a purchase from one of the street dealers once I felt comfortable with how their crew operated. So, on the fourth day I did just that."

"You bought crack?" Coop asked.

"Yessir. Went right up to one of the guys working the corner by my motel and bought a hundred dollars worth of rocks," Clarence confirmed. "I made sure to flash my money roll when I bought it, too."

"How come?"

"Because most crackheads only have enough money to buy enough for a fix. By showing them that I had a thick roll of Benjamins, I was letting them know that I wasn't no crackhead. I made sure that they watched me walk back across the street to my motel, too, because I knew that dude I just bought the rocks from would go back and tell his boys that some new cat with a lot of dough was in the neighborhood."

"Wouldn't that make them suspicious of you though? Or maybe even make you a target to get robbed?" Coop asked.

"That's what I was hoping would happen, Coop…"

"Man, you are straight blowing my mind right now, Clarence! You were bad ass, man!"

"I knew that within the next day they'd either pay me a visit at the motel or wait for me outside to see what was up."

"And, did they?" Coop pressed.

"Yessir," Clarence replied. "That night, as soon as I walked outside the motel, I was confronted by four of them. They made sure to flash the guns they had tucked in their waistbands and ordered me to accompany them down the street to meet with some of the leaders of that crew."

"What'd you do? Man, I'd have been pissin' my pants."

"Oh, don't get me wrong," Clarence replied. "I was scared as hell, but I couldn't let them see it. If I was going to convince these guys that I was a true player, I had to act like one. So, away we went…"

"Did you have your gun on you, just in case?" Coop asked.

"Hell yeah, I was strapped," Clarence chuckled. "A true gangbanger is always strapped, and I made sure they saw that I was packing, too. When we got to the apartment building where the gang's leaders were they patted me down, took my gun and the thousand dollars cash I had on me, and made me sit down across from three mean looking dudes."

"Then what happened?"

"They wanted to know where I was from, what I was doing on the Eastside of Cleveland, and if I ran with a set. I told them that I was from Chicago, and gave them all the details of my backstory - that I wasn't part of a

132

gang in Chicago, but was wanted for trafficking and hiding out in the CLE, hoping to catch on with a new crew while I was in town. They grilled me hard, man, trying to see if I was truly 'Zeus' from Chicago. I told them to go ahead and make some calls to any contacts they might have in law enforcement and that they'd find my warrant, which of course, was fabricated."

"Did they?"

"No clue, but they gave me my gun back and said that if I was serious about slinging rock, that I should come back the next day," Clarence answered. "They kept the cash - said it was like a finder's fee or something. Told me to bring another grand back with me to buy more product and they'd give me a corner to work. Sort of like a trial period to see if I could produce for them. So, the next day, that's what I did..."

"You actually sold crack?" Coop asked, incredulously.

"Hell yeah, I did. Sold so much that first week that they gave me even more responsibility, along with a warning that if I ever crossed them that they'd kill me," Clarence laughed.

"Oh yeah," Coop said in return. "That's hilarious, Clarence..."

"Hey man, listen. I was in deep, and with each week that passed I went a little further down that rabbit hole," Clarence said. "By the time it was all over, I felt more of a connection to Zeus than I did to Clarence."

"How did it end?"

"Eventually, I had enough evidence that I let my handler know, via payphone, that it was time to take them down. I gave them the time and place where we would be the next day when a big shipment was supposed to arrive and let the SWAT team do their thing."

"Were you there when SWAT came in?"

"Yessir, and while the SWAT officers knew that one of us was an undercover cop, they didn't know which one. That way, if I was ever going to go undercover again, my cover wouldn't be blown. So, they stormed in and threw me on the ground just like everyone else. It wasn't until we were booked at the jail that my handlers within the VICE unit discreetly ushered me away," Clarence recalled, almost matter-of-factly.

"Did you ever go undercover again?" Coop asked.

"Nope," Clarence said. "Once was enough for me to know that I didn't want that kind of life for myself, let alone my wife. A few months after

I was back home, we found out that Evelynn was pregnant with our first daughter, Sasha. That's when I knew for sure that I'd never go undercover again."

"I'm sure Miz Walters was happy about that," Coop said.

"That's for sure," Clarence agreed. "It took her awhile to forgive me for putting her through all that though. But, in the end, it made our marriage stronger to know that we could get through something so difficult."

"Suddenly, me being gone for a week and getting paid a lot of money to throw a baseball doesn't seem like such a big sacrifice compared to what you went through," Coop sighed, feeling a little sheepish for the self pity that he had been carrying around.

"I didn't tell you that story for you to compare, Coop," Clarence stated. "A sacrifice is a sacrifice, and believe me, you and Cara are each making one this week. However, you'll have a lot more of those to endure throughout your relationship. As long as you both always remember to take those moments and use them to strengthen your bond, you'll be just fine."

*Late Life*

# 22

Simon Craig loved his job as the concierge at the Westcott Hotel. Sure, there were some difficult guests occasionally, but this was still his dream job. As an undergraduate student studying Hospitality Management at Bowling Green State University, he had always hoped that someday he would end up at The Plaza Hotel in New York City assisting famous guests with their dinner reservations, car service, or anything else that they requested from him.

While the Westcott was Cleveland's crown jewel of luxury hotels, it still was a far cry from The Plaza and the clientele that stayed there. The Westcott catered mostly to wealthy business travelers, while The Plaza simply catered to the wealthy.

*Late Life*

When Cooper Madison moved in to Room 1100, the lone penthouse and only permanent residence at the Westcott, Simon finally had his wish of assisting a high profile client. He had fully expected the baseball star to be a pain in his ass, but he soon discovered that Coop was anything but. In fact, he hardly asked Simon to do anything for him and barely left his suite.

While Simon wasn't much of a sports fan, he knew enough about Cooper Madison to know that he had lost his father in Hurricane Katrina, and that he had moved to Cleveland in an effort to escape the world for awhile. Even though the famous pitcher rarely used his services early on during his time at the Westcott, he had always been so polite and generous to Simon.

It wasn't until Coop began dating Cara Knox, whom Simon had befriended during her time while delivering food to the Westcott for Stucky's Place, that the professional athlete really began to take advantage of his services. He would have Simon make sure that Cara had everything she needed, help him plan romantic nights out on the town, and everything in-between. Simon's efforts were always rewarded in the form of an envelope containing ten $100 bills on the first day of each month, and just last Christmas Coop gifted him a TAG Heuer watch.

138

On this day, however, Simon would've worked for free. Earlier that morning, Coop had called him with specific instructions to help make Cara's evening a little brighter. When Coop informed him what he would be doing, Simon almost dropped the phone.

As he knocked on the door of Suite 1100, he found himself shaking with excitement, mostly because of who was on the other end of the cell phone that he held in his other hand.

"Hey Simon," Cara greeted him after opening the door. When she noticed the cell phone in his hand she asked, "Is everything okay?"

"Yes, everything is very, *very* okay," Simon replied with a giddy look on his face. "I have someone on the phone for you, and I just want you to know before you start talking that this is *not* a prank…"

"Who is it?" Cara asked, confused.

"I think it's best if he tells you himself," Simon grinned as he handed her the phone.

"Hi, this is Cara," she announced with slight trepidation into the phone.

When the caller on the other end began speaking, Cara's eyes grew wide with disbelief. She looked back at Simon and mouthed, "Oh my God."

Simon gave her a nod in return, as if to confirm that this was really happening, and crossed his arms. He loved his job, especially during moments like this.

"Oh my God," Cara said into the phone. That was followed by, "I don't know what to say… Yes, it is my favorite movie… I'm actually just about to watch it for like the twentieth time tonight… I will… Oh my God, thank you so much… This is so crazy… Thank you so much for calling… I will… Okay, you have a good night, too… Bye!"

Cara, looking like she just saw a ghost, handed the phone back to Simon.

"Surprise!" Simon said with a laugh.

"Oh my God, Simon," she said, grabbing him by the shoulders. "Did that really just happen?"

"It certainly did," he confirmed.

"Did you do this?"

"No," Simon replied. "That would be Mr. Madison's handiwork. I just made the call to the number he gave me..."

"I can't believe I just talked to Ryan Gosling!" Cara shrieked as she hugged Simon and the two began to jump up and down.

"I know, right!" Simon gasped, just as excited.

"How did that just happen?" she asked, trying to catch her breath after they finally stopped hopping around like a couple of giddy teenagers.

"So," Simon began before taking a dramatic pause, "Mr. Madison called me this morning from the airport. He said that he had spoken with your brother, Jason, who told him that you were planning on watching 'The Notebook' tonight. I guess Mr. Madison was feeling guilty about leaving you and he wanted to surprise you. Apparently, he called his agent, who then called Ryan Gosling's agent, and they both arranged for it to happen. Mr. Madison then called me back with the phone number and time to call him."

As Simon recounted the story, Cara began to tear up with joy. While she was used to Coop going out of his way for her, this was just too crazy to comprehend. She had been so sad throughout the day after Coop left, yet he had somehow managed to cheer her up, even as he was still sitting on an airplane.

"There's one more thing," Simon added. "Mr. Madison asked that I stay and watch the movie with you tonight. I mean, if that's okay with you…"

"Are you kidding?" Cara replied. "Of course, you can. I was just about to order from Stucky's. Do you want to see if Andrew can join us?"

"Ummm, that's a negative on Andrew," Simon said, referring to his boyfriend of the past two months. "Let's just say I will never date a bartender again, even one as gorgeous as Andrew…"

"Oh no," Cara frowned. "You'll have to tell me all about it while we wait for the food."

"Open up a bottle of wine, girl," Simon sighed as he entered the suite. "I'm going to need it to get through this saga…"

"Do you mind if I call Lucy first?" Cara asked. "If she found out that I talked to Ryan Gosling and didn't call her immediately after, she would probably never speak to me again…"

"You go right ahead, girl," Simon encouraged. "Just make sure to include the masterful work of the best concierge in Cleveland when you do…"

# 23

Cooper Madison always sat in the same seat on the team's charter flights. Like most baseball players, he was a little superstitious, but nothing compared to some of his teammates over the years.

Some of his teammates would go to great lengths to ensure that they didn't anger the "Baseball Gods". Wearing the same socks, without washing them, for every game during a winning streak was shortstop, Chance Sterling's, thing. Eating a handful of popcorn out of a fan's bucket before the first inning of every game was how catcher, Chaz DeLisio, kept the evil forces at bay.

For Coop, it was pretty simple. He always sat in the aisle seat of row 11. When he first came to Cleveland he had to actually buy outfielder, Javier

Gomez, the seat's previous occupant, a $3,800 Rolex Submariner watch for the right to sit there.

Transactions like that were pretty typical in all professional sports, and the most common involved a veteran paying a large sum of money to one of his new teammates for the right to wear his favorite jersey number. One of Coop's teammates in Chicago had once paid a rookie $20,000 so he could wear his lucky number after being dealt to the team in a trade.

The plane had been cruising at 35,000 feet for a good hour before one of the young rookie pitchers on the team, Tyler Keith, summoned up the courage to tap on Coop's shoulder from his seat in row 12. Tyler had been debating the entire flight whether or not he should bother the Cy Young winner, but the veteran pitcher seemed to be very approachable during his short time with the club, so he went for it.

"Can I pick your brain?" Tyler asked after Coop turned around.

"Not sure there's much to pick, but have at it, Rook," Coop replied.

"Is it true that you could've played football at Ohio State?"

"Yessir," Coop confirmed. "I was actually committed to play there, but then Chicago drafted me first overall."

144

"This might be a dumb question," Tyler began, "but, do you ever wonder what would've happened had you chosen to play football?"

"Actually, Rook, it's a good question. I think about it a lot," Coop responded, turning further in his seat towards the aisle to face Tyler. "Don't get me wrong, baseball was definitely the right choice, but I still would've loved to just play one game at the Horseshoe in front of 100,000 fans."

"That would be pretty sweet," Tyler agreed.

"Why do you ask, kid?"

"It's stupid," Tyler said. "I mean, the reason I asked is stupid."

"I'll be the judge of that, Rook," Coop countered. "Let's hear it, or I'll double your next fine in kangaroo court…"

In addition to being the club's best pitcher, Coop also served as the judge of the team's kangaroo court. As the judge, Coop was responsible for hearing his teammates plead their cases for various on-field infractions like missing signs, dropping a routine pop-up, or busting out a home run trot on a ball that ended up being caught 10 feet in front of the fence. At the end of the season, all of the team's fines would usually be donated to charity.

145

"Okay…Okay… When I got drafted out of high school I actually had scholarship offers to almost every big school on the west coast for basketball," Tyler said. "Sometimes I just think about it and I know it sounds stupid, especially now that I'm up in the Majors, but I wonder what would've happened had I played hoops."

"I wondered if you played hoops," Coop replied. "How tall are you, anyways?"

"About 6'8", give or take…"

"What position did you play?"

"I was a center in high school, mostly because we didn't have anyone taller than me, but I would've played small forward in college. I could handle the rock a bit and shoot threes."

"Sounds familiar," Coop laughed. "I played hoops for a few years in high school, too. Same thing with me…"

"What made you choose baseball? I mean, besides being the number one pick in the draft," Tyler chuckled. "I mean, let's say you were drafted in the 12th round, like me. Would you have still picked baseball?"

146

"I would've picked baseball no matter where I was drafted," Coop answered.

"How come?"

"I guess it goes back to my very first year playing little league down in Pass Christian," Coop recalled. "Every season, they would do this big opening ceremony, and all the teams would march out onto the field in their uniforms and they'd play the National Anthem. I just remember how cool I felt in that uniform and how perfect the field looked. The fresh chalk on the baselines and the perfectly manicured grass was magical, man. There's nothing else like it. I was hooked…"

"I get it," Tyler agreed. "We used to do the same thing out in Pasadena, where I grew up."

"Kids are always chasing rainbows, but baseball is a world where you can catch them…" Coop quoted one of his favorite lines.

"Did you just make that up?" Tyler asked.

"I wish, Rook," Coop replied, laughing. "That was Johnny Vander Meer. You need to brush up on the history of the game."

"Who does he play for?"

147

"He *played* for the Reds," Coop corrected. "He was a pitcher, and a damn good one. He's the only big leaguer to ever pitch consecutive no hitters."

"Man, I'd kill to throw just one no-no…" Tyler sighed.

"The key is not trying to throw one, Rook," Coop advised. "It takes a lot of luck and the stars aligning for it to happen. Just focus on only giving the batter one hittable pitch an at-bat, and nothing too hittable. Corners, knees, and hands only. Nothing up over the plate, no hanging breakers. If the ump is giving you an inch off the plate, eat that shit up like a pig at a trough."

"I'll definitely work on that," Tyler laughed. "Any other advice?"

"Yeah," Coop replied. "When you're ready, find a girl that will make you forget about all the cleat chasers waiting outside the hotel on road trips."

"And how will I know where to look for her?" Tyler asked.

"You won't," Coop said in a serious tone. "You'll find each other. When you do, you won't be able to think about anyone else. You won't want to, either. You'll want to call her as soon as you land in a new city before the plane even makes it to the gate, and you'll pass on the hotel bar after the game so you can call her from your hotel room."

148

"Is that what your girl does for you?"

"Sure does," Coop replied. "Don't get me wrong, Rook, it ain't always sunshine and lollipops. But, if she's the one, you'd rather spend a bad day with her than a good day with some chick you met at the bar."

"Sounds pretty good to me," Tyler said.

"It is…"

"Sorry for bothering you, Coop," Tyler said. "But, I appreciate you talking to me."

"Anytime, Rook," Coop smiled. "Get some rest. We got a big week ahead of us."

Tyler sat back in his seat and closed his eyes. He still had to pinch himself when thinking about the fact that he was teammates with *the* Cooper Madison. As he tried to drift off to sleep for the last leg of the flight, he hoped that someday he would have a rookie tapping him on his shoulder and asking for advice.

*Late Life*

## 24

Cleveland Police 1st District Commander Michael "Mick" McCarthy sipped his vodka and cranberry as he sat alone, perched atop a stool at the end of the bar. The Red Lantern, located in Cleveland's historic Kamm's Corners neighborhood on the west side, was walking distance from the house he had managed to hold on to after his messy divorce.

His ex, Zoey, had left him almost three years earlier. Her new man, now her husband, was tall, lean, and handsome. He was a Human Resources Manager with an MBA from Case Western Reserve University's esteemed Weatherhead School of Management. He brought home a salary in the mid-six figures, worked a normal schedule, and didn't find it necessary to drink his job away every night.

Basically, Hunter Hellickson was everything Mick was not.

*Late Life*

Zoey had grown tired of being a cop's wife long before she met "Mr. MBA", as Mick sarcastically called him, at a hot yoga class. The long hours alone, worrying, as she waited for Mick to come home had only been part of the problem. What was worse was that when Mick did finally get home, he was typically drunk and belligerent.

Mick would pride himself on the fact that he never hit his wife, even when he was completely hammered. Zoey could never understand how her husband, whom she did love, at least at one point, could wear that as a badge of honor.

She never felt as if she was Mick's priority in life. So, when the handsome, successful, and slightly younger man started to make it a point to ask her how she was doing at yoga class, that was all it took. Soon, the lovers were skipping hot yoga altogether to sweat it out in a different way at his Lakewood high-rise condominium overlooking Lake Erie.

Mick never noticed the warning signs, despite her attempts to make it so obvious that maybe he would actually react in a way that would show he still cared. Finally, after six months of sneaking around, Mr. MBA had asked her to move in with him.

Armed with the courage that having an escape plan out of her dysfunctional marriage brought with it, she packed up her stuff and left. It took almost two days for Mick to even notice she was gone due to the fact that he had passed out in his driveway that first night before he could even get inside the house to see that she had left.

When Mick finally had realized that Zoey and most of her belongings were gone, he found himself not even caring. To him, all she ever did was bust his balls and spend his money. Sex had become non-existent, and they rarely ever seemed to enjoy each other's company. In a way, Mick was thankful that Mr. MBA had taken Zoey off his hands.

Mick grew to love his newfound bachelorhood. He came and went as he pleased, and since they had no kids, he only had to pay alimony to Zoey for about a year before she officially became Mrs. MBA.

Life was pretty good for Mick. He threw himself into his job during the day and drank his face off every night. He even got laid occasionally, usually after the Red Lantern's closing time when he paired off with whichever female was drunk enough to follow him home.

*Late Life*

On this night, however, there wasn't a single woman at the bar, let alone one who he would be able to charm into following him back to his place. So, Mick decided to go hunting for one, and he knew exactly where to look.

# 25

The team's charter jet, a stretched version of the Boeing 737 known as a B738, had just touched down in Oakland when Coop powered his phone on. He waited anxiously as the phone rang, excited to see if the surprise phone call he had set up for Cara went as planned.

"Hello?" Cara answered.

"Hey girl," said Coop, using his typical greeting.

"Oh, darn, it's you," she giggled. "I was hoping it was Ryan Gosling again…"

"Ouch!" Coop laughed. "I'm starting to question if setting up that phone call was a good idea now…"

"You know I'm just kidding," Cara reassured. "But, if you ever slip up, I'm pretty sure I could snag him."

"I will definitely watch my step then…"

"Simon's here," Cara said. "He told me all about how you set the whole thing up. I must say, you certainly know how to make a girl happy, Cooper Madison."

"That was the plan," Coop replied. "Tell Simon I appreciate all his help."

"I will…"

"What are y'all up to?"

"Well, we just finished watching my new BFF's movie," Cara said. "Along with our second bottle of wine…"

"Atta girl," Coop chuckled.

"Are you in Oakland?"

"Yes, ma'am," Coop confirmed. "We'll be headin' to the team hotel soon."

"Are you excited to pitch tomorrow? Lucy and I will be watching the game here."

"I'm fixin' to give 'em the business tomorrow," replied Coop. "Want to set the tone for the road trip with a win."

156

"Well, I hope you're *fixin'* to get some sleep tonight then," Cara mused.

"I'm gonna try," Coop said. "But I hate these west coast trips. It's still light out here, but my body's on Cleveland time."

"At least you have your own room," Cara replied, referencing the fact that veteran ballplayers like Coop typically were given their own hotel room on road trips.

In Coop's case, it was usually a suite. Each hotel the team stayed at also had a concierge whose sole purpose during their stay was to make sure that the players had everything they needed. For pitchers like Coop, who would only appear in one or two games during their stay, that often included scheduling tee times on the golf course at a nearby country club on their off days.

"We're staying at the Hilton by the airport," Coop said. "They always take care of me there, so I'm sure I'll have a nice room."

"Only the best for the sexiest pitcher in baseball," Cara replied playfully.

157

"Thank God Ryan Gosling doesn't play baseball," Coop laughed, his words causing one of his teammates to give him a confused look as they stood to get their overhead luggage. "Hey, we're about to get off this bird and head to the hotel. I'll call you in the morning?"

"You better…"

"Love you," Coop said.

"I love you more," Cara replied.

# 26

Cleveland's Detroit-Shoreway neighborhood on the West Side had become a hotbed for prostitution over the past few years. Aside from the occasional undercover sting operation to give the impression that the department had the problem under control, the area located near Edgewater Park was known as a prime location for a desperate man to find the company of a woman.

Mick parked his unmarked cruiser on West 83rd Street between Detroit Avenue and Lake Avenue, not far from the shores of Lake Erie. He knew that he couldn't just roll up to a prostitute in an unmarked police cruiser without raising red flags. The working women of the Detroit-Shoreway were pros and knew how to spot an undercover cop, even if he wasn't in a cruiser, so Mick decided to approach one on foot.

*Late Life*

He had spent the past hour after leaving the Red Lantern cruising the area, hoping to find a target that was working solo. So many of the women worked in groups, not only for their own protection, but because it was easier for their pimps to keep an eye on them.

Mick knew, however, that not all of the prostitutes working the area had a pimp. Some were simply women so desperate for money that they found themselves standing on the corner as a last resort.

A slender blonde had caught his attention near the corner of Detroit and 81st. She was likely in her late 20's and was wearing a tight red miniskirt with a sheer black tank top that barely veiled her red bra.

The fact that she kept rubbing her arms as she paced back and forth in a 10 foot area of the sidewalk, while doing her best to look enticing to possible clients, made her a desirable candidate for Mick. She was likely a drug addict looking to score some fast cash to pay for her next fix, but most importantly, she was all alone.

She didn't appear to notice Mick approaching until he was within 10 feet of her. Even when she did, she played it cool as she took a cigarette out of a pack and began to nervously flick a bright pink disposable lighter.

"Ugh," she groaned as the lighter repeatedly only produced a brief spark. "Work, you piece of crap!"

Mick stopped a few feet short of the woman and smirked at her as she grew more frustrated.

"Are you enjoying yourself?" she snapped at him.

"Not as much as I'd like to be," Mick replied, making his intentions obvious.

"I don't mess with walkers," she sighed. "No car, no date. Now leave me alone. You're scaring away the guys who actually own a car…"

"Well, then," Mick began as he extended his hand, which held a Zippo lighter, and cooly lit her cigarette for her. "Good thing I have a car right around the corner."

"I've heard that before, pal," she replied, annoyed, before taking a long drag of her cigarette. "But thanks for the light."

"What's your name? Or should I just call you Gorgeous?" Mick asked, undeterred.

"Cherry…"

"Like the fruit?"

161

"Nothing gets by you…"

"You're a feisty one, aren't you?" Mick laughed.

"Only when I'm annoyed," she sighed, turning her back slightly to him.

"Jeez," Mick replied, pulling out a money clip with a fat roll of cash. "I guess I should take my business elsewhere…"

The sight of the shiny brass clip stuffed with bills caught her attention.

"I told you, I don't mess with walkers," she reiterated. "Even if they're flashing a huge stack."

"And I told you," Mick countered, reaching into his pocket and producing his car keys. "I have a car parked around the corner."

"Then why the hell didn't you just pull up in it instead of walking over here to waste my time?" she fired back.

"I prefer to see the merchandise up close," Mick answered. "I've been fooled before. One time I pulled up on a broad, and only when she got into my car, I realized she had an Adam's Apple…"

162

That made Cherry laugh. She turned towards Mick and batted her eyes.

"Well, I'm all woman…"

"Yes, you certainly are, Miss Cherry," Mick chuckled. "So, are we gonna go back to my car and have some fun, or what?"

"That depends…"

"On what?"

"What you want to do when we get there. I ain't cheap…"

"Neither am I," Mick said, waving the money clip.

"Prove it," she challenged. "It's a hundred up front for me to walk to the car with you."

"That's an expensive walk!" Mick exclaimed.

"I told you, I ain't cheap…"

"I guess not! What about when we get to the car?"

"Another hundred for 20 minutes…"

"What if I take longer than 20 minutes? I prefer to take my time, you know," Mick said, his tone confident.

"Another hundred for every 20 minutes after that," she replied, seductively biting her bottom lip. "But, I'll warn you, I've never had a guy last more than 10 minutes..."

"Is that a challenge?"

"Damn straight it is..."

"I'm game," Mick asserted, peeling off a hundred dollar bill from his clip and waving it it front of her face.

Cherry snatched the crisp bill and seductively tucked it into the front of her tight mini-skirt. "Let's go then, Big Spender..."

They hadn't taken more than a few steps when two unmarked police cruisers emerged from a nearby side street, blue lights flashing from their dashboards. The cruisers came to a screeching halt, one stopping on the side of the street and the other pulling up onto the wide sidewalk to block their progress.

"What the hell?" Mick said in disbelief.

Cherry took a step back as two officers emerged from their respective cars, guns drawn, as they shouted for Mick to get on the ground.

"You're under arrest for solicitation of a prostitute," the first officer announced.

As the officer began reading him his rights, Mick stared at Cherry in shock and disbelief, wondering how he was unaware of the sting. Even though this wasn't his district, as the commander of the neighboring precinct, he should've been given the heads-up that there was going to be an operation.

"McCarthy?" the second officer asked, seemingly just as surprised to see the veteran officer.

"Holy shit… is that Mick?" the first officer asked in disbelief, slowly lowering his gun. "What the hell are you doing out here?"

"Wait," Cherry interrupted. "This guy's a cop?"

"Commander Mick McCarthy, 1st District," Mick sighed.

Mick had always known that a situation like this could happen, and if it ever did, he had rehearsed a plan in his head that he hoped would get him out of the jam. He took a deep breath, collected himself, and went into damage control mode.

"Sorry guys," Mick began, trying his best to sound in control of the situation. "I was heading home earlier and I saw her hooking on the corner. I figured that I'd make an arrest. I was going to call it in to 2nd District once we got back to my cruiser. In hindsight, I guess I should've called it in before I approached her…"

"I want to believe you, Mick," the first officer replied. "But, I gotta ask why you would even bother? I mean, there's always girls working this street. Why would you stop tonight?"

"I guess I could also ask why the hell I didn't know you were running an operation tonight?" Mick countered, tactfully avoiding the officer's question by asking one of his own. "What ever happened to professional courtesy?"

"Hey, your precinct has done plenty of operations without giving us a heads-up, too," the first officer snapped back, holstering his gun.

"You're right," Mick admitted, seizing the opportunity to keep the focus away from why he decided to randomly bust a prostitute. "We all could do a better job of communicating, I suppose."

"Well, this operation is blown now," the second officer said, shoving his gun back into his holster with disgust. "Let's wrap this up."

"Guess I got dressed up for nothing," the woman posing as Cherry sighed.

"The good news is, you were really believable," Mick laughed, before asking, "Are you an officer?"

"Dispatcher," she replied. "Jenn Collins, 2nd District."

"Listen, I'm really sorry about all this. If you want, I'll call your commander tomorrow and explain everything," Mick offered.

"That won't be necessary, Commander," the first officer said. "I think it'll be best if we all just agree to keep this under wraps, since we both could've communicated this better."

"I'd say that I have to agree with you," Mick replied, relieved. "What's your name, officer?"

"Jack Simmons," the first officer replied, shaking Mick's hand.

"Tony Maddocks," the other officer offered, also shaking Mick's hand.

"Again, fellas, and Miss Collins," Mick said with a nod, "I'm really sorry about all this. Next time, I'll make sure to call it in. I guess I was just looking for some action. It's been pretty uneventful for me since the EPK case."

"That was a hell of a job you and Knox did on that case, sir," Simmons asserted.

"Yeah, I'd kill to close a case like that," Maddocks agreed.

"Be careful what you wish for," Mick laughed. "Or you'll become an adrenaline junkie like me trying to bust prostitutes when you're off-duty."

With that, Mick wished the trio the best of luck and instructed them that if they ever needed anything to call him first. They, too, offered the same to Mick.

As he walked back to his cruiser, Mick marveled at his ability to get out of what could have been a very bad situation. He didn't even care if Simmons and Maddocks did end up telling their superior about the incident.

Mick knows that he should've at least felt some sort of remorse or embarrassment, but he didn't. He felt... alive.

# 27

Hannah LaMarca was still feeling the endorphins coursing through her veins as she strolled down Euclid Avenue. She had just finished a workout at the historic Cleveland Athletic Club, and the gentle breeze coming off of Lake Erie felt perfect. She had decided to use a vacation day for the first time since taking over the weekday evening anchor role, and instead of going somewhere out of town, she had decided to use the time as a much needed week of self-care.

The CAC, founded in the early 1900's, was bereft of many of the luxuries that newer workout facilities boasted, but Hannah adored the vintage 15 story building and all of the history that had occurred within its walls. There were rumblings that the club was in serious financial trouble and possibly facing bankruptcy, but Hannah continued to hold out hope that it would find a way to keep its doors open.

Hannah was on her way to The Clevelander Bar and Grill, which was just a short distance from the athletic club, to meet up with a guy that she had been set up with on a blind date. Romance had taken a back seat to Hannah's career, despite her mother's insistence that she find a future husband, but she had agreed to meet this guy because of who had orchestrated the match.

Over the past six months, Keri Urban had gone from being Hannah's contact in the coroner's office, where she played a vital role in helping the young reporter during the EPK case, to one of Hannah's best friends. So, when Keri had informed her that she had someone that Hannah just had to meet, she agreed.

"He's not a coroner, is he?" Hannah had asked two nights prior as the pair shared lunch at Slyman's Deli. "No offense, but I don't think I can date a guy who touches dead people all day…"

"None taken," Keri laughed. "But, no, he's not a coroner."

"But he does have a job, right?"

"Yes, he has a job..." Keri rolled her eyes. "Do you really think I would set you up with a deadbeat?"

"I'm sorry," Hannah apologized. "Blind dates just make me nervous..."

"I get it," Kerri said. "But, this is a good one. I promise."

"Well, are you going to tell me more about him or do I have to use my extensive investigative reporting skills to get it out of you?" Hannah pressed.

"Okay, okay," Keri relented. "His name is Eric Gulden and he's your age. He's an elementary school teacher in Lakewood - first grade, isn't that adorable? So, you know he's got a good heart. He's also an assistant football coach at the high school there."

"So far, so good," Hannah replied. "How do you know him?"

"He played football with my younger brother, Chad, at JCU," Keri said, referring to John Carroll University. "He played tight end there."

"Does he have a tight end, too?" Hannah teased.

"Um, for sure," Keri confirmed. "He's tall, muscular, and absolutely gorgeous..."

171

"Seems too good to be true," Hannah said, narrowing her eyes. "What's the catch? I mean, there has to be a reason that someone like that hasn't been snatched up yet, right?

"Couldn't the same be said about you though?" Keri countered.

"Fair enough…"

"He had a girlfriend all through college, but they broke up when she moved to New York for some job. I guess he's dated a little since, but nothing serious."

Hannah smiled as she recalled the conversation that led her to where she was now, outside the entrance to The Clevelander. She took a deep breath, and walked inside to locate her date using the description that Keri had given her.

The bar was pretty empty, so he wasn't hard to find as he sat at a table along the outside of the trendy establishment. He was wearing a casual buttoned down plaid shirt and jeans. When he noticed Hannah, he stood up, gave a wave, and smiled.

Keri was right - he was gorgeous. And tall, at least 6'3", Hannah guessed as she approached him. He had dirty blonde hair that was trimmed neatly, a tan complexion, and warm hazel eyes.

"Hello," he said as he reached out to shake her hand.

"Hi," Hannah said as she shook his hand in return. "I'm assuming you're Eric, right?"

"That's me," he chuckled, nervously. "Please, have a seat."

Eric, to her surprise, circled around Hannah and pulled out her chair for her to sit down.

"Oh," she said. "Thank you. I guess chivalry isn't dead after all…"

"Well, considering I spend a good part of my day teaching manners to first graders, I'd be a pretty big hypocrite if I didn't practice what I preached," he laughed as he sat down across from her.

"Don't take this the wrong way," Hannah began, "But, you don't exactly fit the mold of a first grade teacher. Those kids must think you're a giant."

"I get that a lot," he mused. "The kids are always a little hesitant at first, but I like to think that I do a pretty good job of getting on their level."

173

"What made you want to teach first grade?" Hannah asked.

"To be honest, it wasn't really my initial plan," Eric replied. "I actually thought I would want to teach fourth grade, but my first student teaching experience in college was in a first grade classroom, and I just kinda fell in love with it."

"Well, I bet they all love you," she said. "They probably don't get many male teachers until they're in middle school. I know I didn't have a male teacher until I was in 7th grade."

"I'm definitely the exception to the rule, at least in our school. I'm the only male teacher in the building aside from the PE teacher."

"Keri said that you also coach football at Lakewood High?"

"Yep," Eric replied. "I coach the tight ends and receivers."

"That's probably a big adjustment every day," Hannah said. "Going from teaching 7-year-olds to high school kids."

"It certainly is, but I like to think that I get the best of both worlds," Eric replied as a server approached their table to take their drink orders.

After the server left with their order, it was Eric's turn to ask some questions of Hannah. He had wrestled all day with what he would ask her

174

about, namely because he felt as though he already knew her from watching her nightly broadcasts on Channel One.

"So," Eric began, "I have to ask something…"

Hannah felt uneasy as he spoke. It was always easier for her to ask the questions than answer them.

"Go ahead," she replied.

"When was the last time you spoke to someone you had just met, and they didn't ask you the same fifty questions about your job as a television reporter that you probably get tired of answering?"

"Oh," Hannah replied, a little caught off guard. "Come to think of it, I can't really remember the last time that happened."

"Well then," Eric said, "here's my promise to you. I'm not going to ask you anything about your job…"

"Okay," Hannah said in return, a little suspiciously. "But, aren't you curious, at all?"

"To be honest, I'd rather get to know Hannah, the person, first," he asserted, looking her in the eyes. "My guess is that she's pretty amazing, and because of that, she ended up with the job that she has…"

*Late Life*

Over the next two hours, Eric Gulden made good on his promise. They talked about their childhoods, their families, and even divulged their most embarrassing teenage moments. When Eric tried to pay the tab, the owner of The Clevelander said that he refused to charge *the* Hannah LaMarca for drinks at his establishment, which led to Eric teasing her about that as he walked her back to her apartment in downtown Cleveland.

By the time that they had reached the door to her building, Hannah felt as if she had just spent the evening with an old friend. Eric was funny and smart, but most importantly, he didn't try too hard to be either.

"So," Eric asked as they stood outside her building. "Would you be interested in going out with me again sometime?"

"I would love that," Hannah smiled.

"Me too," Eric said.

"Then, it's a date," Hannah replied. "Call me tomorrow?"

"Count on it," Eric promised.

The two shared a brief, friendly embrace. However, both felt as though the next time they held each other that it would be as more than just friends.

# 28

"Did you bring me anything?" Gabby Knox asked her father as he walked through the front door of their modest home on Cleveland's west side after his second day back on the job.

"What, I don't even get a hug hello anymore?" he replied, feigning disappointment with his hands on his hips.

Gabby ran and jumped into her father's arms and squeezed him tight. No matter how many times the two played this game, he hoped that there would never be a day without it.

"Hey, Dad, guess what?" Gabby whispered into her father's ear as he carried her toward the kitchen.

"Chicken butt?" Jason whispered back.

"No, silly!" Gabby squealed.

"Well, you got me then. What?"

"It's Taco Tuesday!" Gabby shrieked, followed by the song that she always sang on taco night. "It's Taco Tooooozday! It's Taco Tooooozday!"

"Only if you go wash your hands first, Senorita," Erica warned as she greeted her husband with a kiss.

Gabby hopped out of Jason's arms and ran towards the bathroom, all while she continued to sing her ode to tacos.

"Thank God she has my singing voice," Jason declared in jest, as anyone who knew Erica also knew that she had once been the lead singer of a local bar band in her 20's.

"Well, she's definitely your daughter," Erica replied, purposely ignoring his commentary on Gabby's musical talents. "Her school called today…"

"Oh, so you're saying this was a good call then," Jason said, hoping he was right, but knowing that the opposite was likely true.

"Can you be serious for just a second?" Erica snapped.

"You're right," Jason relented. "I'm sorry. What did they say?"

178

"Well, apparently our daughter went on the internet at school and printed off an article on the EPK case to use during 'Show and Tell' time today…"

"Oh man…"

"Exactly," Erica confirmed. "By the time the teacher realized what was going on, Gabby had already told the entire class about how her daddy helped catch the notorious Edgewater Park Killer."

"She's just proud of her old man, though right?" Jason responded. "I mean, that's not as bad as I thought it was going to be."

"I agree," Erica said before adding, "except for the fact that two kids left the class crying because they were terrified that another serial killer could be on the loose."

"Ahh, I see…" Jason said sheepishly. "Did you talk to her about it yet?"

"Not yet, I wanted to wait for you. I figured we could talk about it during dinner."

Jason sighed before asking, "Just so we are on the same page, we aren't actually mad at her over this, are we? I mean, she will need to understand going forward why it isn't appropriate to talk about serial killers at school, but I really don't want her to feel bad for being proud of me. This job takes me away from you guys enough as it is, and the last thing I want is for her to resent it for another reason."

"I can live with that," Erica replied. "As long as she understands that something like this can never happen again."

"Fair enough," Jason agreed. "Do you want to play the good cop or the bad cop this time?"

"How about you play the good cop now, but later tonight you play the bad cop?" Erica instructed, her tone suggestive.

"Should I bring my handcuffs?" Jason played along, not realizing that Gabby had just entered the kitchen.

"Handcuffs? Are you going to arrest someone tonight, Daddy?" she asked enthusiastically, yet oblivious to the reason her father was discussing handcuffs.

"No, sweetie," Erica interjected just as Jason was stumbling over his words while trying to come up with an appropriate lie. "Daddy knows that tonight is Taco Tuesday."

"That's right, Gabby girl. We are going to eat some tacos and then watch Coop play baseball on TV. How does that sound?" Jason followed up, hoping that the thought of Erica's delicious tacos and baseball were distracting enough to permanently change the subject.

It seemed to do the trick, because Gabby started singing, "It's Taco Tooooozday! It's Taco Tooooozday!"

Jason looked to his wife, who had a look of relief on her face. He loved that he had Erica by his side to weather all of life's storms. He would never be able to accurately describe just how much he loved her, but he had vowed on their wedding day that he would never stop trying to show her in every other way.

*Late Life*

# 29

"Oh my God, I missed you so much!" Lucy Eckert exclaimed as she wrapped Cara up in an enthusiastic embrace just steps inside Suite 1100 at the Westcott Hotel.

"We just talked on the phone last night, and you just saw me at the funeral last week, LuLu," Cara laughed, squeezing her friend tightly.

"And your point is?" Lucy countered, smiling. "I mean, can't a girl just miss seeing her BFF anymore?"

"You're right," Cara chuckled. "I missed you, too."

"So, are you going to tell me about your phone call with my future husband, Ryan Gosling?" Lucy asked.

"I already told you everything last night when I called," Cara laughed.

"Maybe I want to hear it again? Oh, hey, look what I brought for us to enjoy while we watch the game," Lucy said, pulling a bottle of Boone's Farm Strawberry Wine.

"Oh my God, I haven't had this since-"

"The lake house after prom!" the pair declared, almost in unison.

"What did that set you back? Three bucks?" Cara mocked.

"Only the best for us!" Lucy asserted. "Besides, I will need it to watch an entire baseball game on TV. Even if your man is pitching..."

"C'mon, it's not that boring," Cara replied. "Besides, you know you like watching all those athletes running around in their tight pants."

"It'll be the closest I've come to seeing a male physique in weeks," Lucy sighed.

"I'm really sorry to hear about you and Colton," Cara said sincerely.

"I guess it just wasn't meant to be," Lucy shrugged. "C'mon, let's open up this cheap wine, and I'll give you all the details before the game starts."

The two spent the next hour sitting at the kitchen table as they worked on the bottle of wine and Lucy told Cara all about her most recent breakup.

Colton Finn, the heir to a wealthy furniture store family who Lucy had met at Oberlin, had seemed like a great boyfriend for the first few months they were together.

He was handsome, intelligent, and absolutely doted on Lucy. Most importantly, Cara approved of him, despite the fact that Coop felt otherwise.

"That boy thinks the sun comes up just to hear him crow," Coop insisted one evening after the two couples went on a double date.

"No, he doesn't," Cara defended. "Is he a little vain? Sure. But, he absolutely adores Lucy, and that's all that matters."

"If you say so…"

It irked Cara, as Lucy gave her version of the breakup, that Coop was right about Colton. However, she also knew that her judgement was likely clouded because she just wanted her friend to be happy.

Lucy's emotions alternated from sadness to anger as she recounted the evening that she caught her Cinema Studies major boyfriend in a tryst with a freshman theatre major when she showed up unannounced at his apartment.

*Late Life*

Her evening class had been cancelled at the last minute, so Lucy picked up food from their favorite restaurant and decided to surprise Colton, who had told her that he was going to be working on a term paper all evening.

"The dumbass didn't even lock his own apartment door!" Lucy exclaimed as she relived the encounter. "The best part is that when I walked in on them going at it on the living room couch, he tried telling me that they were just rehearsing lines for a project."

"No, he didn't!" Cara laughed.

"Yes, he did!" Lucy shouted, still in disbelief at his lame excuse.

"What did you do?"

Lucy sighed, then said, "I threw the food at him and wished the very naive, very naked, freshman girl good luck with her inevitable porn career. Then I left... for good."

"As you should have!" Cara exclaimed. "Screw him! He doesn't deserve you, Lu..."

"I'll drink to that," Lucy agreed, raising her glass.

"Amen," Cara seconded as the two clinked glasses.

"Enough about my failed love life," Lucy said, changing the subject. "How have you and Coop been doing?"

"Great," Cara replied. "I mean, the past two weeks have been really challenging, but he's been so amazing. Not just to me, but to everyone. Especially my mom. Coop made sure that everything was handled as far as the funeral home was concerned, and he spent two days helping my brothers go through my dad's stuff."

"Not gonna lie, Carebear, but you hit the freaking lottery with that one," Lucy chuckled. "I'll admit, I was skeptical at first. I just figured that he'd be like all the other professional athletes you read about, but he actually seems to be a genuine guy."

"He is…"

"Not to mention he is gorgeous," Lucy added.

"He certainly is," Cara sighed.

"I am curious about something very important, though," Lucy said, her tone measured and stoic.

"Okay?" Cara replied, shifting nervously in her seat.

"Does he swing a big bat in the bedroom?"

"Oh my God, Lulu!" Cara laughed. "I thought you were going to ask something serious!"

"Who says I'm not being serious?" Lucy responded, feigning shock. "Inquiring minds want to know if he knows his way around the bases, Miss Knox...."

"You're such a dork," Cara sighed. "C'mon, the game's about to start. Maybe you can pick out which of Coop's single teammates you'd want him to set you up with..."

# 30

"Hey, Madison!" bellowed an Oakland fan as he leaned over the metal rail located near the visitor's bullpen along the first base side of the stadium. "I know you can hear me, Madison! You suck!"

Although he would never acknowledge the obnoxious fan, Coop could, in fact, hear him. Thanks to the fact that Oakland was one of the last ballparks to have their bullpen located on the field of play, albeit in foul territory, visiting pitchers were often serenaded with vulgarities as they warmed up within a few feet of the fans.

"Hey, Madison!" the fan shouted, undeterred by Coop's lack of acknowledgment. "I heard that Cara's dad died so he wouldn't have to watch you pitch ever again!"

*Late Life*

Coop resisted the urge to turn towards the fan. Every single fiber in him wanted to turn and fire a 97 mile per hour fastball at the guy's head, but he wasn't going to give this guy the satisfaction.

He had heard far worse over the years, especially in New York and Philadelphia. One time, a fan in Philly almost got him to snap without saying a word. Instead of hurling verbal insults at Coop, he simply sat in the front row behind home plate and held up a large poster that had a picture of the pitcher's late mother on it.

When his old manager with the Cubs, Skip Parsons, asked Coop if he wanted to have ballpark security kick the guy out, he declined. Instead, he used it as motivation to pitch a complete game shutout. After he threw the final out, Coop looked over to where the man had been sitting, only to find an empty seat.

"Guys like that are cowards, Coop," Skip had said after the game. "And every single one of them would trade their worthless lives for yours in a heartbeat. Always remember that, Coop…"

Coop gave a nod to his catcher, Chaz DeLisio, signaling that he was done with his warm-up. The veteran catcher popped up out of his crouch and jogged over to Coop.

"Don't listen to that asshole," Chaz said into his glove, just as all battery mates did during mound visits, in the event someone was reading lips.

"Don't even know what you're talking about, CD," Coop replied, also into his glove, with a wink.

"Atta boy," Chaz nodded. "Locked in…"

"I feel good tonight, CD," Coop declared.

"Yeah, I can tell. Fastball is popping and your yakker is sharp, brother," Chaz agreed, referencing Coop's slider.

"Hard stuff early and often then 'Mr. Snappy' when we're ahead in the count," Coop advised, using the nickname given to his slider by Chaz after they began playing together last season.

"Sounds like a plan," Chaz replied. "If they start squaring up the fastball, we'll pitch you backwards second time through the order."

"I don't think we'll need to worry about them catching up to my fastball today, CD," Coop said confidently, as he placed a hand on the catcher's shoulder.

"It's your world, Coop. The rest of us are just paying rent tonight," Chaz laughed as the two began to walk towards the visiting dugout.

As they began their stroll, the fan doubled-down on his efforts to get a reaction out of Coop.

"Hey, Madison! Where's Cara?" the fan screamed. "Oh wait, I know! She's back in Cleveland getting banged by a bunch of dudes!"

Chaz started to turn towards the fan when Coop stopped him.

"Don't," Coop ordered. "That's what he wants, CD."

"You're right," Chaz relented with a sigh. "But, if you change your mind, just let me know. It'll be worth the fine and suspension to curb stomp that prick…"

"I have a better idea, CD," Coop said. "Why don't you go yard in your first at-bat, then I'll take it from there. I'm only going to need one run tonight…"

"Deal," Chaz replied. "I could use a dinger, anyways. Haven't been able to barrel a ball up in over a week."

"That's because you overthink things at the plate," Coop said in return. "I've never seen someone obsess over his swing as much as you do. You know what you need to do at the plate tonight?"

"Normally, I wouldn't take advice on hitting from a damn pitcher, but I'm desperate," Chaz sighed. "Go for it…"

"Forget all that crap that you and every hitting coach love to talk about. Launch angles, exit velocity, and all that other bullshit," Coop insisted. "Instead, take the Pete Rose approach tonight."

"The Pete Rose approach?" Chaz asked, visibly confused.

"See ball… Hit ball…" Coop answered.

Chaz shook his head and laughed as they descended the steps into the dugout.

"It's that easy, huh?" the catcher asked as he strapped on his batting gloves.

*Late Life*

"4,256 hits can't be wrong, CD," Coop mused as he sat in his usual spot on the far end of the bench, leaned back, and pulled the brim of his hat down over his eyes.

Just as he always had done before every game during his career, Coop closed his eyes and began visualizing each batter that he would face. His teammates and coaches knew to never interrupt him during this mental exercise, going as far as to not come within ten feet of him in the dugout prior to taking the field.

On this night, just as always, Coop prepared his mind to block out everything except the task at hand. While he realized that tonight's game would just be a momentary escape from the realities that awaited him after his last pitch was thrown, it didn't prevent him from feeling a slight tinge of guilt over the fact that he was blessed to have this reprieve while Cara was back at home and dealing with the loss of her father, alone.

Coop decided that he would do everything in his power to pitch in a way that would help her take a little bit of the hurt away, even if only temporarily.

Tonight he would pitch for Cara.

194

# 31

*Cooper Madison enters the bottom of the 9th inning here in Oakland as he tries to achieve what so few have ever done before by throwing a perfect game. The veteran flamethrower has been dominant all evening, retiring every batter he has faced by relying on his potent two pitch arsenal.*

*Since returning from Tommy John surgery last season, Madison's fastball has developed what they like to refer to as having 'late life' as it seems to actually pick up velocity before reaching home plate. He has used that to his advantage tonight, stymying hitters early in the count by placing his fastball on both sides of the plate, and then shutting the door on them by unleashing his devastating slider, which catcher Chaz DeLisio has named 'Mr. Snappy'.*

*DeLisio has had quite a night for himself, not only behind the plate, but also in the batter's box. The veteran backstop is a perfect 3-for-3 this*

*evening, including a solo home run in the top of the first inning to put*
*Cleveland up on top one to nothing, which is where the score still stands as we*
*head into what could be the final frame…*

Cara sat frozen on the couch with her hands squeezed tight, afraid to move, as she listened to the television announcer recap what was shaping up to be Coop's finest outing as a major leaguer. Once she realized that the possibility of a perfect game was in reach during the 7th inning, Cara let her own superstitions take over as she watched the rest of the broadcast.

Despite the fact that her bladder told her otherwise, Cara suppressed the urge to use the bathroom, fearing that if she moved out of her seat on the couch, she would somehow impact the outcome of the game.

"Can I get you something to drink, Carebear?" Lucy teased, knowing that her best friend was doing everything in her power not to sprint to the bathroom.

"You're evil, Lulu," Cara replied through gritted teeth.

"C'mon, please tell me that you don't honestly believe that if you go pee that the universe will punish your boyfriend…"

"I told you," Cara snapped back. "I'm *not* moving…"

"Okay, okay… I'll stop," Lucy surrendered. "But, only because I love you…"

*Madison winds and delivers the first pitch of the inning… It's a pop-fly fouled back behind the plate… DeLisio throws his mask off… He's camped under it, and… Makes the catch! One pitch, one out here in the bottom of the ninth…"*

"Holy crap!" Cara exclaimed, squeezing her hands even tighter.

"The catcher guy is kinda cute," Lucy offered as the camera zoomed in on Chaz DeLisio, his smiling face one of relief after making the catch.

"He's married," Cara replied.

"Happily?" asked Lucy, to which Cara only responded to by rolling her eyes.

"Just watch the game; we can play matchmaker later," Cara quipped.

*Vazquez steps into the box for the third time tonight… He grounded out his first time up and went down looking back in the sixth… Madison takes the sign… Winds and delivers… Swing and a miss, strike one… That last fastball was clocked at 97… Here comes the 0-1 offering… Vazquez connects and sends a fly ball deep to center… Bradley is retreating back towards the wall… And makes the catch!*

Cara let out a sigh of relief after realizing that the catch had been made for out number two. When the ball was hit she thought for sure it was a home run and closed her eyes, unable to watch.

"C'mon, Coop! One more out!" Lucy yelled at the television, much to Cara's surprise, as she had never seen her friend so involved in the outcome of a game.

*Cooper Madison is now one out away from throwing a perfect game, just one year after undergoing Tommy John surgery… Billy Snyder digs in… He's grounded out twice today… Snyder actually has a career batting average against Madison at just over .300… You have to assume if anyone has a shot at breaking it up, it would be Snyder… Madison rocks and fires… Swing and a miss! Strike one… Looks like the catcher DeLisio called for a slider, and I don't think Snyder could've been fooled any more than he was on that pitch… Madison starts his wind-up… And Snyder fouls that one straight back for strike two… Wow, Snyder was all over that fastball and just missed possibly ending Madison's bid for a perfect game… It looks like Chaz DeLisio has asked the umpire for time and is now trotting out to have a chat with his pitcher...*

"I don't know why you're running out here, CD," Coop spoke into his glove. "You and I both know what I'm throwing next..."

"Hell, Coop, everybody on the planet knows you're throwing a slider," Chaz laughed.

"Then why the hell are you out here?"

"Well," Chaz began, "I just wanted to say thanks for giving me this experience. I mean, I've caught a lot of great games, but this has been unlike anything I've ever seen..."

"Hey, CD, you know we still have to get this last out, right?" a confused Coop asked.

"Yeah man, that's why I wanted to thank you now," Chaz replied, slapping Coop on the shoulder. "Because in about thirty seconds after you strike this guy out, the place is going to go nuts. I mean, it's gonna be crazy, and I wanted to thank you before all hell breaks loose..."

"Oh...." Coop responded. "Well, I guess you're welcome then?"

"Good. Glad we got that out of the way," Chaz acknowledged with a wink. "Now strike this asshole out so we can party. You're buying…"

Coop laughed and nodded as Chaz gave him a quick pat on the ass and then trotted back towards the plate.

*I'm assuming after that last pitch that the catcher, Chaz DeLisio, wanted to discuss their approach with two strikes here… Madison looks in for the sign… Nods… Starts his wind-up… And here's the 0-2 pitch… Swiiiiiiiing and a miss! Strike three! Cooper Madison has just pitched a perfect game! His teammates are swarming him on the mound! Cooper Madison has just achieved baseball immortality, folks…*

"Oh my God!" Lucy screamed as she jumped up and down on the couch. "He did it, Carebear!"

Cara was bursting with joy on the inside as tears of joy streamed down her face. While she knew that staying back in Cleveland was the right decision, Cara couldn't help but feel a little sadness creep in. She wished that she could jump into the TV screen and join the throngs of teammates who were all taking turns giving their star pitcher a congratulatory embrace.

# 32

Jason was just about to finally nod off to sleep after staying up late to watch Coop make history when his phone began to vibrate from its place on his nightstand. He turned to make sure that it had not awakened Erica, who despite their playful banter about handcuffs, had crashed in the third inning, and he was relieved to see that she was still fast asleep.

Seeing that it was Mick, he answered in a whispered tone as he quietly exited the bedroom.

"Hey, Mick. What's up?"

"That was a hell of a game, man!" Mick exclaimed.

"Sure was," Jason replied in a hushed tone, hoping that Mick would take the hint.

It must have worked because Mick said, "Oh crap, did I wake you up? I just figured you guys would still be up because of the game."

"Well, Erica and Gabby are both out like a light, but I was still somewhat conscious when I heard my phone vibrating."

"If there were  any doubts that Coop's a Hall of Famer, I think that he just erased them tonight," Mick stated.

"No argument here…"

"Hey, Knox," Mick began.

"Yes…"

"Did anyone happen to say anything to you about a prostitution sting the other night over in 2nd District?" Mick asked, purposely not specifying the exact day.

Perplexed, Jason responded, "Prostitution sting? Can't say I've heard anything. Why do you ask?"

"Just curious," Mick answered.

"Is it something you want me to look into?" Jason asked, trying to make sense of where his commander was going with this conversation.

"No, it's all good," Mick assured him. "I just had heard that they might've been running an operation and typically they'd give us a heads-up, but I never was told anything."

"Well, I have no problem giving them a call tomorrow to find out, if you'd like," Jason offered.

"Nah, like I said, it's all good. I'd rather keep it on the down low that we're aware so we can hold it over their heads later if need be," Mick chuckled.

"Copy that," Jason affirmed.

While he thought it was odd that Mick would even care about a prostitution sting, even one without the proper professional courtesy, he chalked it up to Mick just being a control freak, as usual. In the time since his divorce, Mick had seemed to throw himself into his job more than ever, which in their line of work wasn't necessarily a bad thing.

"Hey, I'll see you in the morning. Get some sleep," Mick said.

"Will do, Mick. See you tomorrow."

As Mick plopped down in his worn leather recliner, he took a sip of decaf coffee from what had become his favorite mug. To the casual observer, it was just a white porcelain cup with a simple blue logo from a Las Vegas casino gift shop.

To Mick, however, it was a daily reminder of so much more.

*Late Life*

# 33

Coop tried calling Cara's phone for a third time, only to have it go straight to voicemail again. He had just finished giving interviews and was still in his uniform when he had grabbed his cell phone out of his locker to call her.

His phone had more than 30 voicemails and another 50 or so text messages from everyone except the person who he had wanted to hear from the most.

Coop realized that it was really late back in Cleveland and that maybe she had fallen asleep, but still he had really wanted to share the greatest individual performance of his career with her. Hopefully, he thought to himself, she had at least stayed up long enough to watch it.

He had placed the phone back on the shelf of his locker and began to undress when a call came through. He quickly grabbed the phone and felt a tinge of sadness when he saw that the call was not from Cara, but rather it was his agent Todd "T-Squared" Taylor.

Coop answered the call, "What's up, T?"

"Uh, yes, can you get me Mister Perfect, please?" Todd asked.

"Pretty wild, huh?" Coop responded.

"You're damn straight, Coop!" Todd enthusiastically agreed. "You have just cemented yourself in baseball immortality, my man! Are you going out to celebrate, or what?"

"Yeah, CD already called and rented out the VIP room at some club," Coop replied. "To be honest, I'm so drained that I just want to go back to my hotel room, order room service, and crash. But, I'm pretty sure that the guys would kill me if I did that…"

"As they should, Coop," Todd concurred. "This may never happen again, not just for you, but for any of your teammates who got to be a part of it today."

"I know. That's why I'm going…"

"Listen, you tell CD that I am covering the tab tonight," Todd implored. "Just tell him to fax me the receipt and I'll handle it."

"You don't have to do that, T," Coop said, though he was flattered that his agent would be so kind.

"Like hell I don't," Todd replied. "Besides, when we negotiate your next contract, tonight's performance will more than make up for what I'm about to spend."

"Fair enough," Coop chuckled.

"Have you talked to Cara yet?" Todd asked.

"No, actually," Coop sighed. "I think she might've fallen asleep. It's pretty late back in Cleveland. Speaking of time zones, where the heck are you calling from this time?"

"I'm actually back home in Florida, sitting out by my pool. Joy and the baby are sleeping," Todd said in response.

"I never thought I'd see the day," Coop mused. "Todd 'T-Squared' Taylor… family man…"

"I wouldn't want it any other way, brother," Todd asserted sincerely.

"I know you wouldn't, T," Coop agreed.

207

"Alright, now quit talking to me and get out there with your boys to celebrate your big night!"

The two old friends said their goodbyes, and Coop headed to the showers. As the hot water cascaded over his body, he couldn't help but feel as though something was definitely not right with Cara's lack of communication after the game.

"Hey Coop!" Chaz DeLisio's voice bellowed from just outside the showers. "Let's go, brother! We're about to turn it up!"

"Hell yeah, we are, CD!" Coop yelled back.

# 34

Mick couldn't sleep after his phone call with Jason.

This was not out of the ordinary for the veteran cop since his divorce, which is why he usually did everything in his power to drink himself to sleep every night. One of the benefits from hanging out at establishments like the Red Lantern was that in addition to tying one on, he would sometimes bring home a female companion to help fill the hours that should have been occupied by sleep.

It was during those late night encounters, however, that Mick still found himself feeling unfulfilled. The void that he was trying to fill wasn't sexual in nature.

If that was the case, he never would've visited Buddy's Speakeasy.

He never would've met Vivian Tong.

*Late Life*

The empty feeling that left Mick wanting something more than a closing time hookup is what had led him to Buddy's.

As an officer of the law, he had dedicated his life to upholding it. His tireless approach to law enforcement is what compelled him to work long hours and drink away the evils that he encountered on the job every night.

In Mick's mind, his devotion to upholding the law cost him his marriage, and he resented it. He wanted to get his revenge on the very principles that he had blindly believed in and fill the void that they had left in his soul.

The day that Mick painstakingly created what would become his alter ego by modifying a West Virginia driver's license is when he first felt the emptiness begin to shrink.

It was on that day that Eugene Lankford was born.

Eugene Lankford, Mick determined, would enable him to wander into the abyss that he had spent two decades on the wrong side of a losing battle against.

Eugene Lankford would dance with the devil and take what he wanted without remorse.

During that first night at Buddy's Speakeasy, Mick saw what he wanted. She was a goddess in a sequined thong and when she danced on stage, it was as if she was dancing for only him.

Vivian Tong became his muse, but just like many artists who become enamored with who they thought was a perfect creature, her luster began to wear off. She began acting just like every other woman who had grown tired of him.

She became just like Zoey.

By doing so, she unknowingly gave him an opportunity to fill the hole that years of upholding the law had created.

Mick was certain that he could feel her soul occupy that torturous void as he squeezed the life from her waif-like frame. It was a euphoric transfer of energy. A sensuous waltz with evil.

Mick McCarthy, he determined, would continue to uphold the law just as he always had.

Eugene Lankford, however, would only answer the tempting call of the Siren that had coaxed him from the darkest part of Mick's subconscious.

Evil had become his new muse, and with an irony that only accompanies the most sinister of associations, it had even provided him with the perfect scapegoat for his crime in the form of the EPK.

The killer that he had devoted months to bring to justice would take the fall for Vivian's death. His involvement in the investigation by day would resolve any fear of being caught that might creep in by night.

There had been one person who could have made the connection between Mick and Eugene Lankford, and that was the owner of Buddy's Speakeasy, Vance Gold. Prior to he and Jason's first visit to question Vance about Vivian Tong's murder, Mick had paid him a surprise visit and gave him an offer that he couldn't refuse to keep his mouth shut.

Mick had offered Vance a sum of $100,000 in exchange for his silence, to which the cash-strapped Vance had gladly accepted after Mick had given him the first $10,000 up front.

What Vance didn't know at the time was that the $10,000 Mick had given him was the only money that he would ever see, as Mick had planned to kill him long before any more money would exchange hands. Phil

Worthington, however, had unknowingly saved Mick the trouble on the day he placed a zip-tie around Vance's neck and squeezed the life from his body.

Mick had hoped that the void he had felt had been filled forever when he robbed Vivian Tong of her last breath. That seemed to be the case in the following weeks. In a twisted way, Mick even believed that by taking her life, he had become a better cop because he was no longer trying to satisfy the vacant space in his soul.

The Siren's call, that irresistible melody from his wicked muse, had even vanished. That is, until his sinister temptress provided him the gift of Dolly at the Imperial Palace lounge.

It was on that night that Mick had felt the murderous melody beckon the presence of Eugene Lankford to appear once more. Unlike the mythical enchantresses that Homer spoke of, Mick truly believed that his Siren had reached out to guide, rather than kill him.

She had told him through her sinister song that there was still room in his empty soul for one last kill, and that Dolly would have to surrender hers in order for him to fill it anew.

*Late Life*

# 35

"You know something, Coop? You're my freaking hero, man," Tyler Keith, the young rookie pitcher that Coop had mentored on the plane, declared through slurred words.

Most of Cleveland's team was still inside Oakland's Uptown Nightclub, but the rookie hurler had been "all gas and no brakes" since arriving at the club after the game, and Coop had volunteered to take him back to the team hotel.

"I appreciate that, Rook," Coop chuckled as he guided the youngster to the taxi that had been waiting for them in front of the club.

The Uptown had opened in 2005 and featured a 30 foot historic mahogany bar that had originally been installed at The Old Spaghetti Factory in Jack London Square. The wooden bar was rumored to have traveled through the Panama Canal before landing in Oakland, according to the bar's owners.

"No, man, I mean, like... you're really my hero, man," Tyler reiterated as Coop helped him climb awkwardly into the back seat of the cab.

"Alright, Rook," Coop replied. "You can profess your love to me tomorrow when you're hungover, okay? For now, just focus on not puking on me in the back seat."

Coop's words caught the attention of the cab's driver, who looked as though he was about to kick them out of the car when he realized who one of his passengers was.

"Holy crap, you're Cooper Madison!" the driver exclaimed. "I listened to your game tonight. I'm a Giants fan, so I was rooting for you to get that perfect game!"

"I appreciate that," Coop replied with a smile.

"Man, are the guys going to be jealous when I tell them that I drove THE Cooper Madison tonight," the cabbie declared. "So, you guys staying at the Hilton?"

"Yessir," Coop confirmed.

"I'll get you there safe and sound, Coop," the driver promised before adding, "and don't you worry about your pal there. If he pukes, I'll handle it. No problem…"

"Well, let's hope that dog don't hunt tonight," Coop chuckled as he looked over towards Tyler, who had already passed out.

Coop had enjoyed a few drinks with the team, but he was far from drunk. He couldn't shake the feeling that something more was wrong with Cara. He had even tried calling her two more times from the bar, even at the risk of waking her up in the middle of the night, but her phone had gone straight to voicemail on both attempts.

There was another reason that Coop had decided to leave the club early and he hoped that he was overreacting to the situation, but his gut told him otherwise. Word had traveled fast that an entire professional baseball team had been partying at the Uptown, so the club was packed that evening.

Coop's teammates had done their best to insulate him from the typical interactions with the bar's patrons, but he had managed to oblige a few autograph requests and even posed for a few photographs.

For the most part, those who approached him were respectful and polite. However, when he posed for one last picture, something occurred that had the potential to be an issue for Coop as two scantily clad young women and the young man they were with decided to make the most of an impromptu photo op with a celebrity athlete.

The girls, who appeared to be in their early twenties, had approached Coop and begged him for a picture. He had lived long enough in the public eye to know that posing for a picture with anyone, let alone two attractive and provocatively dressed young women, could potentially lead to trouble.

One time, a few years earlier, Coop was approached by a sharply dressed man in the lobby of a hotel in Alabama and asked to pose for a photograph. Coop assumed that the man was probably a lawyer or a CEO based off of the tailored suit he was wearing, so when the man asked him if he would give a "thumbs up" to the camera, he didn't give it a second thought.

About a week after the photo was taken, Coop's "thumbs up" picture began making the rounds on every news channel in the country. As it turned out, the man that he had taken the picture with was the Grand Wizard of the largest Ku Klux Klan chapter in the southeastern United States.

Coop, who had always despised anyone with racist views, was furious. Thankfully, Todd Taylor had jumped all over it, initiating damage control, and within a week most of the country knew that Coop had been the victim of circumstance. Regardless, it bothered him to know that there were people out there who likely still believed that he was associated with the KKK.

As the taxi made its way back to the team hotel, Coop replayed the encounter with the two young ladies over and over in his head, trying to convince himself that it was likely nothing to worry about. He knew that he hadn't done anything wrong, but if that picture went public, the damage that it would cause could become catastrophic.

*Late Life*

# 36

Mick sat in his old leather recliner and sipped a vodka and cranberry. He had given up on trying to sleep and figured that the alcohol would help numb the feeling that maybe he hadn't been as careful as he assumed he had on that night in Las Vegas.

The Imperial Palace Hotel and Casino was not a place that the "Vegas elite" frequented. Most of the hotel's 2,600 rooms were rundown and were more comparable to a cheap motel than a resort located in the heart of the Las Vegas Strip.

The "IP" had always catered to the middle-class gambler, with low table limits and daily rates that were typically half the cost of its neighbors on the Strip. Those weren't the reasons why it was Mick's favorite place to gamble though.

*Late Life*

Mick, who had inherited the same gigantic chip that his father had carried around on his shoulder, loved gambling at the IP because it was one of the few places in Vegas where he felt like he was more successful than the majority of the clientele. It was for that reason that Mick had found himself at the IP the previous October.

"So, Mister Eugene Lankford... are we going to my room or yours?" the woman who called herself Rebecca had asked Mick.

"I thought you'd never ask," Mick replied.

"Well, I just had to," she purred. "I got tired of waiting for you to..."

"I'm sorry," he apologized. "I guess I've never been very good at reading women."

"It's okay. I have a few ideas on how you can make it up to me..."

"I'd love to take you to my suite," he said, before leaning in to whisper, "It's really... really... big..."

"Oh my," she cooed.

"Are you up for a drive?"

"A drive?" she asked, surprised. "Aren't you staying here?"

"No," he lied. "I'm actually a VIP at the Red Rock. I prefer to stay off the Strip. You ever been there?"

"No," she replied. "But I hear it's beautiful."

The Red Rock Casino Resort and Spa had just opened a year earlier and was the latest in a line of grandiose resorts that had become popular in the areas surrounding Las Vegas. Located 20 minutes west of the Strip in Summerlin South, Nevada, it featured nearly 800 rooms and had a tremendous view of Red Rock Canyon. Guests could experience everything that Las Vegas had to offer, without the congestion that accompanied the casinos on the Strip.

"It is beautiful," Mick confirmed. "Just like you…"

"You certainly know how to make me feel that way," she said.

"Oh, I'm just getting started…"

"How far away is it?"

"Only about 20 minutes, but totally worth the drive. They comped me with a suite that overlooks Red Rock Canyon."

"Comped?" she asked. "Wow, you must be a high roller…"

"I told you," he replied. "I'm a VIP, baby…"

"Do you mind if I just run up to my room real quick? I want to freshen up a bit and grab a couple things before we go."

"I'll tell you what," Mick said as he brushed her drugstore dye job black hair away from her ear and gave her a soft kiss on the cheek. "You go on up to your room and do what you have to do. I'll get my car from the valet and wait for you out front. Look for a silver Lincoln Continental…"

"A Lincoln? Look at you Mister VIP…"

"First class all the way, baby…"

"What are you, some sort of banker or something?" she asked as she stood up.

"Nope," Mick replied with a smirk as he stood, pulled out his money clip, peeled off a $50 bill, and placed it on the bar.

"What do you do then?" she asked as she pressed her chest against his.

"Let's just say that the people I work for prefer that I don't discuss my profession," he answered, telling the truth.

"So mysterious…"

"If I told you, I'd have to kill you…"

# 37

Dolly hummed as she gave herself one last look in the mirror before leaving her room at the Imperial Palace to meet Eugene Lankford by the valet stand. She didn't give a second thought to jumping into a car with a complete stranger that she had just met an hour earlier. Besides, she knew that it was him that should have been more cautious.

While she had always had a thing for bald guys, she had no intention of sleeping with Eugene once they made it back to his suite at the Red Rock. This was going to be a business trip.

She had already blown through the majority of the cash that she had taken from Phil Worthington back in Tennessee, and she needed another quick score before hitting the road again. Vegas had served its purpose, but she had already been there much longer than she had originally planned to be. In order to survive, she would need to get some cash and leave town to stay one step ahead of the authorities.

Dolly had been a survivor her entire life.

Constance Eleanor Boggs, Dolly's true identity, was born in Kay Moor, West Virginia. Kay Moor, sometimes spelled Kaymoor, was one of the many mining towns in the Mountain State that time had left behind.

Like so many of the West Virginia coal miners of his era, Samuel Boggs had dropped out of school after the 9th grade to start working in the mines, just as his father had before him. He married his childhood sweetheart, Arlene, when they were both only 17 years of age.

Things had started well for Sam. He had a steady paycheck, a one bedroom house not far from the mine, and a wife that he loved waiting for him at the end of every shift. Constance soon followed, and the couple began making plans for more children and a bigger house.

That all changed in 1962 when he became one of the hundreds of coal miners who saw their only means of supporting a family slip away when the mine shut down for good.

Constance, their only child, was just 5 years old at the time. Sam and Arlene had wanted to have more children, but God had other plans, as she became one of the millions of women to suffer from what doctor's referred to as secondary infertility after the birth of her daughter.

With no education to fall back on and zero prospects for a job in Kay Moor, Sam left his young family and enlisted in the United States Marine Corps. Two months later, during a live fire training exercise, Sam was struck in the head by a stray bullet, killing him instantly.

When the news of Sam's death reached Kay Moor, the outpouring of support, along with the military's monetary death compensation given to Arlene and her daughter, sustained them for the first year. But, as time passed, the money dwindled.

Arlene, who did have her high school diploma, decided to pack up what little they had and move north to Cincinnati in search of a better life. They settled into a studio apartment in the Mount Auburn neighborhood of the city.

Arlene found work 6 days a week at one of the local dry cleaners. The paltry pay barely covered the rent, but her schedule did enable her to be home every day when Constance got off the bus from school. On Saturdays, the owner allowed Arlene to bring her daughter with her to work as long as she stayed in the back.

It was during those long Saturdays that Constance learned firsthand how unfair life could be as she watched her mother do all of the work while the owner sat in the back office. A rotund man in his fifties, Stu Blankenship was the epitome of a male chauvinist.

He would scream at Arlene every time she made the smallest of mistakes, even when the fault was his own. Constance would watch Stu berate her mother almost every weekend, wondering why Arlene would put up with such abuse. One Saturday, when Constance was 8, she raised the question as the two walked back to their apartment.

"Why do you let him scream at you like that, Momma?" she had asked.

Arlene stopped dead in her tracks and kneeled down, pulling her daughter's face close to her own, and said something that her daughter would carry with her for the rest of her life.

"I put up with it so that you never will. I want you to learn from my mistakes, Constance Eleanor," Arlene whispered, tears welled up in her eyes.

She gave her daughter a kiss on the cheek, hugged her tight, and then the pair continued their walk home. Constance made a promise to herself that day to never let a man control her. She also made a vow to get back at Stu Blankenship the following Saturday.

Stu was a creature of habit. Every Saturday morning began with a cup of coffee and a toasted bagel with cream cheese from one of the local bakeries. He would always place the styrofoam cup of coffee on his desk and take the lid off to let it cool down while he walked around the front of the shop and ate his bagel.

On this day, Constance, who would typically sit at a small table near his back office and color or read on Saturday mornings, pretended to read a book while she watched him make his way to the front of the shop. Once he was out of eyesight, she produced a spoon and a little plastic bag that contained the powder from the six laxative tablets that she had stolen from her mother's medicine cabinet and crushed into a fine powder.

*Late Life*

She quickly snuck into his office and emptied the entire bag of powder into his coffee, mixed it with the spoon, and retreated back to her desk. Constance didn't feel any remorse as she watched him return and take a long sip from the cup.

Stu, who noticed that the coffee tasted slightly bitter, opened up two sugar packets and emptied them into the cup. After stirring in the sugar, he took another swig and declared to nobody in particular, "Much better…"

Constance did everything in her power to keep a straight face as she watched her mother's tormentor finish the entire cup of coffee. Ten minutes later, Stu was cursing and running out of his office faster than she had ever seen the man move as he made a beeline straight for the small bathroom located near his office.

Twenty minutes of groaning and swearing followed from behind the bathroom door. When Stu finally emerged, he was as pale as the white linens that his store cleaned on a daily basis.

"Arlene!" he yelled toward the front of the shop, "I'm going home for the day. You'll have to lock-up. I think I must've had some bad shellfish last night at the Elks lodge…"

Once Stu was gone, Arlene checked in on her daughter, who was grinning as she colored a picture of a toilet.

Upon seeing her daughter's artwork, Arlene asked, "Is there something you want to tell me, Constance?"

"No, ma'am," her daughter replied, suppressing a laugh.

Arlene narrowed her eyes at her daughter, but chose to leave it at that before returning to the front of the shop to attend to a customer.

Constance continued to color, and with each stroke of her Crayola crayon, she felt the satisfaction of her actions continue to grow. She felt powerful.

She felt alive.

*Late Life*

# 38

Coop was awakened in the predawn hours on the morning after pitching his perfect game by an incoming call on his cell phone. He quickly hopped out of the king sized bed and rushed over to the table where his phone had been charging. It was Cara.

"Hey, girl," he answered as he looked at the alarm clock, which indicated that it was just past four in the morning in Oakland. Coop hoped that Cara had simply forgotten about the time difference and that she wasn't calling because something was wrong.

"Did you have *fun* last night?" Cara asked in an accusatory tone, bypassing any greeting.

Coop, who was still a little foggy due to lack of sleep, replied, "Well, yeah. I mean, it's not every day you get to throw a perfect game."

"I'm not talking about your stupid baseball game, Coop!" Cara yelled.

"Stupid baseball game?" a confused Coop asked as he tried to gauge where the conversation was headed.

"It's all over CMZ, Coop," Cara said, crying. "How could you do this to me?"

"Whoa, whoa, whoa…" Coop responded. "Slow down, girl. Who licked the red off your candy? I have no idea what you're talking about."

"Oh, bullshit!" Cara seethed before adding, "And save your stupid southern sayings."

Coop felt his heart sink as his exhausted brain began to put the pieces together. That's when it hit him that the picture from the club had obviously been leaked to the media.

Before Coop could reply, Cara sneered, "I hope they were worth it."

She had hung up.

Coop immediately called her back, only to have the call go straight to voicemail. He tried again and again.

Nothing.

Coop walked over to the desk in his suite and powered up his laptop computer. He went straight to CMZ's website and saw what he had hoped he wouldn't.

"Coop's Naughty Night Out" was splashed across the top of the page in bold font. Below it was the picture of a smiling Coop standing in between the two girls from the club, one blonde and the other brunette, both of whom had their tongues out. Even though the photo had been censored using two black rectangular boxes, there was no doubt as to what it was that they were concealing.

Coop recalled the moment immediately after the picture was taken when he had realized that each of the girls, without warning, had decided to flash their breasts for the camera. The guy they were with who had taken the picture must have been aware of what was going to happen before he snapped the photo, as he had shown no surprise when the two beauties exposed their chests.

The whole incident had been very well received by the other patrons in the club, including Coop's teammates, who whooped it up and cheered for the brief show. Only Chaz DeLisio seemed to realize the implications that such a picture could cause because he had attempted to confiscate the digital camera from the guy, but to no avail as the young man immediately made a beeline out of the club.

The girls followed suit, leaving a bewildered Coop behind.

"Do you want me to go after them?" Chaz asked.

"No, it's okay, CD," Coop replied. "That'll just make things worse…"

"Maybe he didn't get a good picture," a hopeful CD declared. "It is pretty dark in here."

"Yeah… Let's just hope that this was just for their personal collection," Coop added, trying to stay positive.

Coop felt like an idiot as he stared at the image on his computer. The last thing that Cara needed was to think that he had been anything other than the victim of circumstances beyond his control, but he also knew it really didn't matter if she believed him or not.

The damage had been done, and now it was out there for the world to see.

# 39

Mick's place had slowly transformed into a bachelor pad since Zoey had left him. Baseball paintings, framed movie posters, and vintage tin automobile signs had replaced all of the artwork that his ex had taken such great pride in finding at local art shows.

The early morning sun had crept its way through the curtains of his living room and had cast a natural spotlight on his favorite vintage sign. It was a painting of a 1956 Lincoln Mark II parked in front of a rising outdoor staircase. Mick had always loved the Ford Motor Company's luxury brand of automobile, which is why he would always rent one when in Las Vegas, just as he had on the night he met Dolly.

"Hey there, Big Spender," Mick recalled Dolly greeting him as she sat down in the passenger seat of the silver Continental, which had been waiting for her at the valet stand outside of the Imperial Palace Casino. "Eugene Lankford knows how to travel in style…"

"Well, as beautiful as this Lincoln is, you just made it that much prettier, Rebecca," Mick replied, getting a kick out of being addressed by his alter ego.

"Well, aren't you just a charmer?" Dolly cooed.

"Wait until you see what I have planned for you tonight," Mick declared as he pulled the luxury car away from the IP.

"I was just about to say the same to you," Dolly replied.

As the car made its way down Las Vegas Boulevard, Dolly saw a prostitute standing on the corner at one of the intersections. Most people probably wouldn't have noticed the working girl, she thought to herself, but Dolly could spot one a mile away.

At the age of 18, when she was still known as Constance Eleanor Boggs, she had grown tired of just getting by. She was tired of watching her mom live paycheck to paycheck, tired of wearing clothes from the Salvation Army, and tired of waiting for some good luck to come her way.

So, against Arlene's wishes, she decided to make her own luck a reality by leaving the Queen City for good. Armed with a few hundred dollars, a backpack, and a wealth of resolve, Constance Eleanor Boggs boarded a Greyhound bus that was headed for Nashville, Tennessee.

It didn't take long for the fresh-faced Constance, who had just graduated from high school that May, to land a job as a cocktail waitress for one of Nashville's many country music saloons. After only a few days on the job, the brunette haired Constance noticed that the waitresses with blonde hair seemed to get better tips.

It's not that Constance wasn't attractive in her own right. Her long brown hair accented a body that had more than enough curves to garner plenty of attention from the opposite sex ever since she became a teenager.

Constance, however, didn't just want attention. She wanted money. Lots and lots of money. She had goals to achieve.

A bottle of drugstore hair bleach did the trick. She would typically leave the bar every evening with a wad of cash from the hoards of male customers who thought that an extra ten bucks on their bar tab would increase their chances of taking the young waitress home. Unfortunately for them, she never once took any of them up on the offer.

She had an efficiency apartment that was within walking distance to the bar and had enough money left over at the end of each month to even send some back home to Arlene. The rest went straight to the shoe box that she kept on the top shelf of her closet. Handwritten on the box were the words, "College Fund".

Constance finally felt as if she was winning at life and could actually see herself using the money from that shoe box to pay for a degree in business some day. She fell asleep each night dreaming of a corporate career, complete with her name stenciled on the window of her own corner office.

That dream was put on hold the day that she waited on a 22 year old aspiring country musician named Alan King as he waited to take his turn on stage at her bar's open mic night.

He was tall, dark, and handsome with a deep voice and a charming Georgia accent. Constance, who had always prided herself on never dating a patron, fell head over heels in love with Alan King the moment he called her "Darlin".

All at once, the ambitious young woman who had saved up nearly eight thousand dollars in that shoe box during the two years that she had been in Nashville, found herself spending every waking minute with Alan.

She was front and center at every bar where he was able to play on stage. She began to occasionally call off work to attend his shows, even on the weekends when she would typically make twice the amount in tips as she would during her weekday shifts.

Going out to support her new boyfriend at bars was expensive though, and Alan wasn't actually making any money playing music. Withdrawals from the previously "deposit only" shoe box became a regular occurrence.

Alan, who had been living in his van when he met Constance, had managed to move in with her after just a few weeks of dating. At first, she didn't even care that he contributed next to nothing when it came to the bills. He was an artist, after all, and she truly believed that he was just paying his dues in order to make it someday.

*Late Life*

Three months after they first met, Constance returned home to her apartment after a long shift at the saloon to find that Alan had completely moved out. She was totally caught off guard, as they had rarely even had so much as an argument during their time together.

Despite making that promise to herself as a young girl to never let a man control her destiny, Constance had come to the realization that she had been played by the very first man that she had ever loved. She was crushed.

She was so devastated that it took her nearly two days to even realize that he had also stolen the thousands of dollars that had remained in her shoe box. The note that he left inside the box for her to read simply said, "Sorry…"

She was not only brokenhearted, she was also simply broke, something that she had sworn she would never be again when she left Cincinnati. She was furious with herself.

Things took another turn for the worse during her first night back on the job when a drunk customer slapped her on the rear after placing his drink order. It was not the first time that a customer had done that to her. In fact, it had happened on a pretty regular basis throughout her tenure as a cocktail waitress. Alan King, however, had also stolen her patience for such behavior when he ran off with her money.

Constance quickly turned around, grabbed an empty beer bottle off the table next to her, and smashed it across the man's face. As a result of the retaliation, she was immediately fired from her job and eventually spent a month in jail for the assault.

Once out of jail, Constance returned to her apartment only to realize that she had been evicted during her incarceration. Her landlord informed her that her possessions had been thrown out on the street corner weeks earlier, much to the delight of the city's homeless population, which she had now become a member of.

She had nothing. Again.

Constance knew that she could return home to Cincinnati and move back in with her mother, but her ego wouldn't let her. Attempts to get another waitressing job were also fruitless once the proprietors learned of her assault charge.

After a few weeks of sleeping wherever she could, showering at the YMCA, and begging for food and money on street corners, she was

243

approached by a man who wore a bright yellow suit and referred to himself as Sharky.

While she had never actually met a pimp in person, Constance knew that's exactly what Sharky was. Desperate, hungry, and tired of not sleeping in a real bed, she took him up on his job offer. Sharky had said at the time that there was only one stipulation.

"Girl, we have got to change your name. Ain't no John out there that wants to mess with some broad named *Constance*," Sharky had said as he looked up and down at her blonde hair and ample bust. "Your new name is Dolly, ya dig? You know, like that foxy singer…"

It was on that day that Constance ceased to exist and Dolly was born.

Two long years of working for Sharky came to an abrupt end the day that she plunged a knife into his throat as a retaliation for slapping her the day before when she had refused to turn a trick for a group of men.

Dolly, under the pretense that she was visiting him at his home to apologize, calmly watched Sharky struggle for air as he frantically writhed on the ground, blood spurting out of his jugular.

244

She laughed as he took his last breaths and cursed him so that those would be the last words that he had ever heard in this lifetime. She had seen him open the safe that he kept in his bedroom enough times during her tenure as one of his top earners that she had no problem opening it up and promptly clearing out every cent of the nearly fifteen thousand dollars that he had stashed in there.

Dolly, unlike Alan King, did not leave a note. She did, however, leave the life of a prostitute behind in Nashville as she began her decades-long journey that had led to her riding in the passenger seat of Eugene Lankford's silver Lincoln Continental.

"Whatcha thinking about, Rebecca?" he asked his date for the evening, who seemed to be momentarily lost in thought as they made their way down the Strip.

"Oh, I'm sorry," Dolly replied, slightly embarrassed, before recovering. "I guess I'm just trying to think what it is you have planned for me tonight."

"Soon enough, my dear," Mick promised. "You'll never experience anything like it again for as long as you live…"

*Late Life*

# 40

To anyone who might've caught a glimpse of Dolly's limp figure slumped towards the passenger window of Mick's Lincoln Continental, they likely would've assumed that she was sleeping off a long evening of boozing on the Strip. Even that was unlikely though, since most people traveling Interstate 15 towards Utah at that time of the night were just focusing on staying awake themselves.

They had been about 20 minutes into the drive when Dolly started to question why Mick was heading north instead of west towards the Red Rock Casino, as planned.

"Hey, Sweetie, I think you missed your turn," Dolly had said, with an uneasy laugh.

Mick, staring straight ahead, said nothing in return.

"Uh, excuse me, Eugene?" she tried again.

Mick remained silent, eyes fixed on the road.

"Hey!" Dolly said sharply, snapping her fingers near his face.

Mick calmly checked his rearview mirror and was satisfied to see that there were no other vehicles within a quarter mile of his rented Lincoln. He turned his head and responded to his finger-snapping passenger in a cold, yet calm, tone.

"Don't do that."

"Just what the hell is going on here?" Dolly asked, angrily. "Why aren't we driving to the Red Rock?"

Mick rolled his eyes.

"Hey! Asshole!" she screamed. "I asked you a goddamn question! Answer me before I..."

"Before you *what*?" Mick snapped, his cold eyes challenging her to finish her thought.

Dolly, fully aware by this point that getting in the car with Eugene Lankford was a huge miscalculation on her part, slowly began to reach into her purse.

248

"Listen, pal," she began as her hand cautiously felt for the souvenir buck knife that had never left her possession since purchasing it at a Gatlinburg gift shop. "I don't know what you're up to, but you're messing with the wrong bitch…"

"You see, that's where you're wrong," Mick countered in an amused tone. "I most definitely have the *right* bitch, don't I, *Dolly*?"

His words sent a chill down her spine.

"Just who the hell are you, Mister?" a dumfounded Dolly stammered.

"My name is Commander Mick McCarthy, Cleveland Homicide Division," Mick announced, flashing his badge. "And you, Dolly Barnes, are under arrest."

Dolly, who was still trying to make sense of everything, countered, "I don't know who you think I am, but you have the wrong girl."

"I don't think that someone your age should ever refer to herself as girl, Dolly," Mick laughed.

"Screw you, asshole," she fired back. "I told you that my name is Rebecca. Now, pull this goddamn car over and let me the hell out!"

*Late Life*

Dolly's fingers had finally located the wooden handle of the serrated hunting knife. She firmly clasped her fingers around the smooth handle of the weapon while keeping it out of view inside the oversized handbag that sat on her lap.

"Sorry, Dolly," Mick replied. "That's just not going to happen..."

"Listen here, you fat pathetic loser," Dolly began as she readied the knife inside her purse, waiting for the right time to strike. "If you don't pull over and let me the hell out of this car I'm going to-"

Dolly's words were cut short by a vicious backhand from Mick to the bridge of her nose.

"You talk too much," Mick said to his passenger, who had been knocked unconscious by the blow.

He looked down at the purse on her lap and reached his hand inside, not the least bit surprised to find the buck knife in her limp hand. Mick removed the knife and inspected it in the dim glow of a passing streetlight.

If Mick had any lingering doubts that the woman next to him was anyone other than the infamous "Deadly Dolly", they disappeared as he read the handle which said *Gatlinburg, Tennessee.*

# 41

Erica Knox checked her watch again as Gabby stared out the window. It wasn't like Cara to be late, especially when she was picking her niece up for a fun day at the zoo as they had planned.

"Call her again, Mommy," Gabby said.

"I already have called her three times, sweetie," Erica assured her daughter. "I'm sure that she just overslept. She was probably up really late watching Coop pitch last night."

Erica wished that she could believe her own words, but when every attempt to reach Cara by phone went straight to voicemail, she grew worried that this was something more than just a missed alarm clock.

More than fifty miles away from Erica's house, Lucy Eckert's car cruised south on Interstate 71, with Cara in the passenger seat.

Earlier that morning, Lucy had convinced Cara that an impromptu road trip to Columbus would be the best way for her best friend to deal with the fallout from the CMZ article.

"What about Gabby?" Cara had protested. "I'm supposed to take her to the zoo in less than two hours."

"Just give Erica a call from the road," Lucy said. "She'll understand. You need this, Carebear."

So, the two of them got dressed and hit the road. A shopping trip at Columbus's Easton Town Center was on the agenda, and even Cara had admitted that a little retail therapy was in order. The only problem was that, once on the road, Cara realized that she had left her cell phone back at the Westcott.

"Just use my phone," Lucy had said to Cara, who was cursing the fact that she was going to let her niece down.

"I don't know her number off the top of my head," Cara replied. "Or anyone's for that matter. That's the problem with cell phones; I never know anyone's number anymore. Damn!"

"Then just call your brother at the precinct," Lucy encouraged. "Doesn't every police number end in 1234 or something?"

Cara, having lived in the city throughout college, did know the non-emergency number and dialed it. She asked to be patched through to Detective Jason Knox at the 1st precinct.

Only he wasn't there, so she had left a voicemail for him apologizing for bailing on her scheduled trip to the zoo with Gabby. She added that she hoped that her niece would forgive her.

"Do you want to talk about it?" Lucy asked, referring to the CMZ article.

"What's there to talk about, LuLu?" Cara replied with a dejected sigh.

"Well, for starters, it's not like he was making out with those sluts. I mean, for all we know he didn't even know that they were flashing their boobs."

Cara groaned, "That's not the point..."

"Well, then what is the point?" Lucy countered.

"The point is that he was obviously out at a club and flirting with those girls," Cara answered in a disgusted tone. "He's gone one night and the first chance he gets results in this. It's humiliating!"

Lucy tried to tread lightly with her next words. "That's true. But, he had obviously only gone out to celebrate his big game last night. Was he a dumbass for posing for that picture? Absolutely. But, that doesn't mean that he cheated on you."

"I don't think he cheated on me," Cara countered. "I'm pissed because now everyone *thinks* he did. Do you know what it's like to have everyone on the planet know all of your business? It's exhausting, Lulu."

"No, I certainly don't know what that's like," Lucy acknowledged. "I'll drop it..."

"I'm sorry," Cara sighed. "I just want to escape all of this for the day."

"Fair enough," Lucy agreed. "Just one more thing, though..."

Cara groaned, "Whaaaat?"

"You have way nicer boobs than those two sluts..."

Lucy's words made Cara laugh for the first time that day.

"Oh, I love this song!" Lucy exclaimed as she turned the volume up on the car's radio.

The two best friends belted out the lyrics to Cyndi Lauper's "Girls Just Want to Have Fun" as the car cruised south towards Columbus, and for a brief moment, Cara allowed herself to get lost in the music.

*Late Life*

# 42

Mick placed his handcuffs, badge, and gun back on his bedroom dresser. Despite being fully dressed for work, he had made the decision to phone in sick to the precinct. He had rolled into work half in the bag on many occasions, but after no sleep and a steady stream of vodka and cranberries, he decided not to tempt fate.

Mick stared down at his handcuffs, the same ones he had used since joining the force, and though they had been used to apprehend many criminals over the years it was the one time that they were ever placed on someone outside of the city of Cleveland that came to mind first.

"Welcome back," Mick had chuckled to his prisoner.

Dolly groaned as she came to, but when she tried to bring her hands to her throbbing face, she discovered that they were restrained behind her back. Her feet appeared to be bound together at the ankles as well, and the seat belt was fastened tightly across her chest.

Earlier, about ten minutes after striking her, Mick had pulled over to the side of the road and retrieved the handcuffs from his work bag that was located inside the trunk. While he had already confiscated her knife, Mick knew that someone of Dolly's pedigree would do whatever it took to survive, so he had cuffed her hands behind her unconscious body.

Like many officers, Mick always traveled with his work bag. The bag, which he would declare to airport security with his checked luggage, contained his handcuffs, Glock 9 millimeter, and an array of other items, including a pack of industrial strength zip ties.

"I can't… breathe…" Dolly mumbled as she struggled to free her hands.

"Well, Dolly, that's because I broke your nose," Mick replied, amused. "You can still breathe through your mouth though."

"Cops can't…just… hit someone," Dolly groaned. "I'm going to…report you…"

Mick laughed out loud and replied, "Report me? To whom?"

"Asshole…" she hissed.

"Guilty," Mick agreed.

"Where the hell are you taking me?" she demanded.

Mick said nothing, which only angered his prisoner more.

"I said… where… *the hell*… are you… taking me?" she pressed.

Again, Mick remained silent, grinning as he kept his eyes on the road.

"I'm going to kill you!" Dolly shrieked as she attempted to violently free her body from her restraints, to no avail.

"If I were you, I'd save your energy, Dolly," Mick warned. "We still have a few hours until we get to where we are headed…"

Dolly, though her brain was still foggy from the blow, calmed her body down and spent the next ten minutes silently attempting to deduce where it was that they were headed based on the signs dotted along Interstate 15.

She hoped, based on the direction that they were headed, that he had planned to simply drive her all the way back to Cleveland. She feared, however, as they crossed over the Nevada-Arizona border that he was just driving until he found an isolated place to kill her and leave her body for the local wildlife to consume.

Mick, who had planned on taking a day trip to see Bryce Canyon National Park during his stay, knew exactly where they were headed. He grinned as he recounted his good fortune. Not only would he still get to see Bryce Canyon as the sun came up, but he would also get to answer the Siren's call.

# 43

Dolly wasn't sure just how long she had been asleep when she felt the car come to a stop on what appeared to be a gravel road. Her head was throbbing, and the blood that had earlier oozed from her nose and down her chin from Mick's backhand had dried in an uncomfortable manner around her dry mouth.

"I need... water," she managed to say.

Mick said nothing as he put the car in park, shut the engine off, and exited the vehicle. Dolly opened her eyes to try and figure out where they had stopped.

Prior to fading back into darkness for a second time, Dolly had looked at Mick's fuel gauge, hoping that he would need to stop for gas. If she was lucky, she would be able to attract enough attention to possibly get help.

Unfortunately for Dolly, his tank was still three quarters of the way filled. Even a gas guzzler like a Lincoln could drive for three or four more hours on the highway with that much fuel.

Dolly watched as Mick walked a few feet away from the car, unzipped his pants, and urinated on the ground. It was still very dark outside, but she figured that the sun would be coming up in the next hour or so. She just needed to make it that long.

Mick, who had let out an exaggerated groan of relief as he relieved himself, zipped his pants back up and walked over to Dolly's side of the car and opened her door.

"Man, that felt good!" Mick exclaimed as he grabbed her by her bound ankles and swung her legs towards the open door.

"I need to pee," Dolly said as Mick placed his hands under her armpits and pulled her battered body out of the car. She felt as if her tired legs would give out beneath her as she stood for the first time in hours.

"Then piss your pants," Mick snapped, before adding, "It doesn't matter anymore…"

Dolly felt the terror of what was about to happen wash over her like a tidal wave. She mustered every ounce of strength left in her body and began to scream for help at the top of her lungs.

Mick just laughed, "Don't bother. There's nobody within 20 miles of here, well, except the wildlife. Don't worry, you'll meet them soon enough…"

Dolly ignored his words and continued to frantically scream as she tried desperately to free herself from his grip. She had lied enough in her life to know that he could have been trying to mislead her.

"Okay, that's enough of that," Mick said just before he punched her so hard in her ribs that she heard them crack on impact, causing her to double over and struggle for oxygen.

Mick continued to hold her upright even though her body desperately wanted him to let her fall to the ground.

"I told you, nobody will hear you. Quit being such an annoying bitch," Mick seethed through clenched teeth as he put his hand around her neck.

It was at that point that Dolly realized that he had put a pair of gloves on his hands. There was no doubt left in her mind what his intentions were, so Dolly put all her cards on the table as a matter of survival.

263

"Listen, please…" she begged. "I'll do whatever you want… I'll go down on you… I'll even let you screw me… Anything…"

Mick just laughed.

"Do you really think that I want to screw you?" he taunted. "Don't flatter yourself, Dolly. I mean, maybe twenty years ago, but now? No thanks…"

Defeated, Dolly began to sob uncontrollably.

"Besides," Mick added, "That's not what gets me off. You want to know what really turns me on?"

Dolly shook her head no, but Mick ignored her.

"Watching a dumb bitch like you struggle to take her last breath…"

At once, Mick tossed Dolly to the ground face first before rolling her over onto her back. He stood over her and from behind his back pulled a knife out of his waistband.

It took her a second to realize it was her knife.

"Oh, do you recognize this?" Mick jested, waving it around for her to take in. "Don't worry, I wiped it down after I put these gloves on…"

Dolly just closed her eyes and wept. She could not believe that this was the way it would end. Even if she wanted to fight back, her body would not have let her.

Mick grabbed her by the hair and dragged her away from the car which was parked on the gravel apron along a bend in the road. While he didn't anticipate anyone disturbing them, he knew that he had to work fast in order to be sure.

He had pulled her limp body into a small batch of Great Basin Bristlecone Pine trees. Once he had determined that she was far enough off the road and out of sight, he let go of her hair and stood over her.

From his back pocket, Mick retrieved a large plastic zip tie that he then looped over her head. The clicking sound of the zip tie's locking mechanism as it slowly tightened around Dolly's neck made his body tingle with anticipation of the kill.

Mick stopped pulling on the zip tie when it was just tight enough to make it difficult for her to breathe, but not tight enough to completely cut-off her oxygen supply.

Dolly was just about to put up one last fight against her attacker when he stood up and kicked her in her already broken ribs. She gasped for air, but between the zip tie and the most recent damage to her ribs, there was no air to be found.

"Shhhhh," Mick whispered as he straddled her midsection and placed his weight on top of her battered body.

Dolly's eyes widened in horror as he grabbed her chin with his left hand and forced her to watch him slowly press the buck knife about an inch into her chest. The pain was excruciating and Dolly prayed for a quick ending.

Mick, however, was enjoying the kill far too much to grant her that wish. He wanted her to feel every inch of the serrated blade as it slowly entered her chest cavity.

Dolly opened her mouth and tried to scream, but the knife had already made its way into her lung. Mick held her chin tightly as he maintained eye contact with her.

He wanted to be the last thing she saw on this planet.

Mick slowly twisted the knife once it had reached its maximum depth and watched as the woman known as "Deadly Dolly" drew her last breath.

The Siren's call had been answered.

An hour later, Mick sat and admired the sunrise as it washed over the natural amphitheaters of Bryce Canyon National Park. He had made sure that Dolly's body was tucked away far enough that it would not be found anytime soon, not even by the local wildlife, save for dumb luck.

Still, he knew that one day she would eventually be discovered, but Mick was just as confident that she would fall into the one-third of unsolved murder cases in America every year.

As he gazed at the rocky landscape before him, Mick fought the urge to go back and check Dolly's body one last time for any signs of evidence that he might have accidentally overlooked. He had done a thorough job searching her and had planned on disposing her purse somewhere that it would never be found on his way back to the resort, but he still couldn't shake the feeling that this would come back to haunt him later.

*Late Life*

# 44

"Okay, here's the plan," Todd "T-Squared" Taylor said from the veranda of his mansion on Casey Key Road in Nokomis, Florida. "First, and foremost, we're going to issue a statement immediately to provide your side of this whole 'Girls Gone Wild' picture fiasco. We're going to make sure everyone knows that you're the victim here, Coop…"

Coop listened as his agent went on to describe the next steps of his plan which involved a phone call to CMZ to pressure them into running a follow-up story in exchange for an exclusive interview with another one of Todd's clients that CMZ had been begging to get. The client, a recently retired professional basketball player, had just come out of the closet publicly, but had yet to do an interview with any major media outlets.

"Is he going to be okay with doing that, T?" Coop had asked.

"Coop, you should know me well enough by now to know that I wouldn't even be telling you if I hadn't already talked to the man," Todd scoffed. "He's actually been wanting to do an interview. I just had to convince him that CMZ would be the best place to do it, which in reality, it is. It'll reach a far wider audience than ESPN or any of the other traditional outlets."

For the first time that day, Coop began to feel a little better about the entire situation, which is why Todd was the first person he had called after speaking with Cara that morning.

"I appreciate it, T," Coop replied. "I hope you know that…"

"C'mon, brother. This is what I do," Todd reassured his top client. "Besides, this is nothing in the grand scheme of things."

"Tell that to Cara," Coop sighed.

"She'll be fine, Coop. Trust me…"

"I have to see her, T," Coop asserted. "In person…"

"Not a problem," Todd responded immediately. "I'm going to put you on a private jet back to Cleveland today. You don't pitch for another five days, so it shouldn't be an issue. I'll call management as soon as we get off the phone and grease those wheels a little to make sure. Besides, you just threw a freaking perfect game. You could go to Vegas for the next four nights, and they wouldn't give a crap."

"Thanks, T," a grateful Coop said.

"Anything for you, Coop," replied Todd. "Can you be packed and ready to go to the airport in an hour? I'll send a car."

"Absolutely," confirmed Coop.

A few minutes later as Coop unzipped the outer pocket of his suitcase, he discovered a folded piece of paper that he had not noticed when unpacking his bags two nights earlier. He unfolded the note and immediately recognized the handwriting as belonging to Cara.

*Coop,*

*I hope you find this before your game. I just want to tell you how much I love you and appreciate how you have been there for me, not just these past two weeks, but throughout our entire journey together.*

*I'm so proud of how hard you have worked to get back on the field after your surgery, and I know that you'll do great out there!*

*Late Life*

*Please don't worry about me while you're gone, even though I know*

*you will. I will be counting down the days until you get back!*

*Love,*

*Cara*

*P.S. "Nothing"*


Coop's heart sank as he read the note. Cara was angry and he couldn't

blame her, even though he also knew that he had done nothing wrong.

Regardless, he was determined to make things right, even if it meant leaving

his teammates in the middle of a road trip to do so.

# 45

Detective Jason Knox was exhausted.

He had stayed up late the night before to watch Coop throw a perfect game, fielded a phone call from Mick in the middle of the night right at the moment he was about to fall asleep, and then tossed and turned until his alarm went off. To make matters worse, once he arrived at work, he was told that Mick had phoned in sick.

Jason had seen Mick show up to work religiously, especially since his divorce, even when he was battling a cold or a vicious hangover from one of his many late nights at The Red Lantern bar, so it was a bit of a surprise to the detective when his commander was a no show. He had been just about to call and check up on Mick when a surprise visitor showed up at the precinct.

"Detective Knox?" the man standing in the door to his office had asked.

The man was tall, lean, and sported a navy polo shirt with a circular badge stitched on the chest. Jason didn't need to read the words stitched around the outside of the badge to know that it was the logo of the United States Marshals Service.

"That would be me," Jason confirmed as he stood to greet the man.

"Brad Coreno," the man said as they shook hands.

"Oh, wow," Jason said, a little caught off guard. "I didn't even realize you were in town."

"There's a reason for that," the Marshal informed in a hushed tone. "Can we talk in private?"

"Of course," Jason said as he invited him into his office and closed the door.

Brad took a seat at one of the two wooden chairs that sat in front of Jason's desk as Jason made his way back to his worn leather office chair. Brad looked around the sparsely decorated office and then back at the door to make sure that nobody was within earshot.

The Marshal took a deep breath and began, "Listen, Jason, I'm sorry for the unannounced visit, but I'll explain everything."

"No apologies are necessary, Brad," Jason answered, waving it off. "So, what brings you to the C-L-E?"

"At the risk of sounding cliché," Brad paused before finishing his thought, "I have some good news and some not so good news."

Jason leaned forward in his chair and said, "Go on…"

"Well, the good news is that we have some surveillance footage from the Imperial Palace Casino in Las Vegas that we are pretty sure shows our Jane Doe leaving the premises with a man whom we believe may be responsible for her death," Brad conveyed.

"Whoa," a surprised Jason said in response. "How the heck did you know to check those specific cameras?"

"Well, I'd love to say that it was the result of some crack investigative work on my part, but I'd be lying," Brad mused. "The reality is that the killer was extremely thorough in making sure that he didn't leave any evidence behind, at least none that could be found without the help of DNA experts, and we are still a couple weeks away from getting those results."

"So, what was the break you caught then?" Jason asked.

"This," Brad said as he produced a manilla envelope and retrieved a photograph from it before he handed it to Jason. "It was folded up and tucked inside the watch pocket of the victim's jeans."

Jason looked at the color photograph which displayed an image of a slot machine payout voucher for $20.18. At the top of the receipt was the logo of the Imperial Palace Casino and a date and time stamp.

"What the hell is a watch pocket?" Jason asked, his eyes still fixated on the image of the receipt.

"You know that tiny pocket that's usually located right above the main pocket on a pair of jeans?" Brad asked.

"Actually, yeah, I do," Jason chuckled. "I always wondered what the heck that was for. Seems useless…"

"Well, in today's world, it pretty much is," Brad agreed. "But, back in the day it was to hold a pocket watch. Thankfully, the makers of the victim's pair of jeans decided to keep the tradition alive; otherwise, we wouldn't have found that. The killer had likely gone through all of her pockets, with the

276

exception of the now infamous watch pocket, before abandoning the body because we didn't find anything else at the scene."

"That's insane," was all that Jason could say in return as he shook his head in disbelief.

"So, we went to the Imperial Palace and started looking over all of the footage of the slot machines that they had from the date and time of the voucher and there she was," Brad informed as he handed Jason three more photographs.

The first image showed a curvy middle-aged woman with frizzy black hair, tight jeans, and a revealing top sitting at a penny slot machine. The next two showed her sitting alone at a bar.

"How did these images compare to the video from the gift shop in Gatlinburg?" Jason asked as he shuffled the photographs in his hand.

"Aside from the change in hair color, it's undoubtedly the same woman," Brad confirmed.

Jason, who finally had a face to go along with the woman that had eluded authorities for so long, stared at the images as the reality set in. He had always imagined what she would look like based on the descriptions given by eye witnesses, and while they had been very accurate, the image in his mind had always made her out to be more menacing than the woman he saw in those photographs.

"Well, that's great!" Jason said excitedly. "What about the suspect? Do you have any leads on him?"

Brad took a deep breath and then exhaled. He produced one more photograph from the manilla folder, and as he handed it over to Jason, he said, "You tell me…"

To say that Jason was shocked to see an image of Mick sitting at a bar with Dolly would be an understatement of epic proportions. He even tried to hold the picture closer to his face in hopes that maybe it was just someone who looked like his commander, but all that did was confirm that it was indeed Mick.

"I… don't understand…" was all that Jason managed to say as he continued to stare at the image in front of him.

"That is Commander Mick McCarthy, correct?" Brad asked.

"Yes, but…" Jason began as he looked up at Brad. "You don't really think that Mick…"

278

"We do, Jason," Brad said in a sincere tone, knowing that he had just shattered everything that Jason had thought he knew about his partner and friend. "In fact, here are some more stills from the surveillance videos."

Jason, almost reluctantly, accepted the photographs from Brad and began to look through them as the disbelief inside him continued to fester. Each image he viewed that clearly showed Mick seemed to squash any hope that maybe this was just a coincidence.

"When were these taken?" Jason asked.

"October 21st of last year, which was exactly when-"

Jason finished his sentence, "Mick was in Vegas…"

"Correct," Brad agreed.

"How long have you had these?" Jason asked, still dumbfounded.

"Actually, we just received them late last night," Brad replied. "We hopped on a plane and came straight here. We were actually going to present them to Mick in person here at the precinct, but when we realized that he had called off work, we decided to go with Plan B."

"Which is?" Jason countered.

Brad smiled and said, "Well, Jason, that's where you come in. We sent a couple of our guys from the Marshal Service over to keep an eye on his house this morning while we wait for a federal judge to issue a search warrant for his house. We should have that in our hands within the hour. The plan is that you would call Mick and tell him that you're stopping over with a few Deputy Marshals to discuss the Dolly case. Once he answers the door, we'll serve him with the warrant and search his house."

"Jesus, my head is spinning," Jason admitted. "I just can't wrap my head around any of this. I mean, I've known the guy better than anyone for years. Sure, he's been going through some crap since his divorce, but he's a damn good cop, Brad."

"I don't doubt any of that, Jason," Brad concurred. "But, sometimes even damn good cops go bad."

Jason didn't disagree, but instead asked, "Do you think Mick knew that Dolly was going to be in Vegas?"

"Not sure. For all we know, maybe Commander McCarthy realized that it was her after they left the casino together, tried to place her into custody, and things went south. Dolly is, or was, a very violent woman.

Perhaps Mick accidentally killed her during a struggle, panicked, and then tried to cover it up…"

"This is just insane…" Jason proclaimed in utter disbelief. "Does anyone else in the department know about this?"

Brad shook his head and said, "Just you. To be quite honest, based on recent events, we don't have a whole lot of confidence in the leadership of your department…"

Jason, thinking of the debacle with the late Chief Horace Johnston, replied, "We sure have been putting the fun in dysfunctional recently…"

"Aside from the issues with his divorce, has Mick shown any bizarre or suspicious behaviors recently?" Brad asked.

Jason wanted to say no, but after Mick's phone call the night before, he knew that he couldn't. So, he told Brad all about the phone call and Mick's questions about the prostitution sting and how it just seemed off.

Before Brad could ask any follow-up questions his cell phone rang. He told Jason that he'd be right back and then stepped out of the office to take the call.

*Late Life*

    "The judge issued the warrant," Brad informed as he returned a few minutes later. "You ready to roll?"

    Jason wanted to tell the Marshal to go without him. He wanted to wake up from what he had hoped was just an unimaginable nightmare. However, he knew that the only option was to go.

# 46

After calling in sick earlier that morning, Mick felt as if he could finally get some sleep after being awake for more than the past 24 hours. The alcohol had finally started to wear off and he had just finished a big plate of scrambled eggs, bacon, and toast - one of the only meals that he knew how to make.

It was as he began to close the curtains of his bedroom window when Mick noticed what appeared to be an unmarked police SUV with a government plate sitting just down the street from his driveway, only he knew right away that the car didn't belong to his department because Cleveland Police did not own any black Chevy Suburbans.

*Late Life*

Mick retrieved the set of binoculars from the top drawer of his nightstand, which he always kept close by in the event that the young woman who liked to sunbathe in her driveway across the street made an appearance.

As he tried to remain hidden from view, Mick used the binoculars to zoom in on the license plate for a closer look, which only confirmed that they were indeed government plates. He slowly scanned up to the windshield and saw that there were two males, both dressed in navy windbreakers and sunglasses, and that one was talking into a cell phone.

Mick's heart sank as he got a closer look at the circular emblem on the chest of the man in the passenger seat. It was the logo of the United States Marshal Service, a group that he had worked with many times over the years in an effort to apprehend violent fugitives.

He kept the binoculars fixated on the two men as his mind raced through every possible scenario on why they were there. While he had hoped that it was just a coincidence and that they were possibly doing surveillance on one of his neighbors, he knew that was just wishful thinking.

They were here to watch him.

Mick felt a small flash of hope enter his thoughts as he processed the fact that if they wanted to do anything other than watch his house that they would've already made a move. That hope quickly vanished as he recalled during his days helping the Marshals that they never did surveillance on a suspect unless they had a clear cut motive to.

Mick made the decision that he wouldn't be there to find out, and he immediately went to the closet and grabbed his bugout bag. The concept of the survival kit-style bag had been around for decades, though it had become far more popular since 9/11 when people started to prepare for what they would do in the event of a large scale terrorist attack.

That wasn't why Mick had a bugout bag though. He had first purchased the backpack in the days after he took Vivian Tong's life in the event that he would ever need to go on the run.

Mick slung his bag, which contained a day's worth of food and water, a thousand dollars in cash, a change of clothes, a hunting knife, and extra ammunition for his Glock, over his shoulder before grabbing his gun, badge, and handcuffs from the dresser and made his way downstairs.

*Late Life*

After he took a peek through the keyhole of his front door and saw that the SUV was still in the same spot, Mick moved to the kitchen which was located in the back of the house and contained the only other door that one could use to gain entry.

Like most of the bungalows that lined the streets of his West Park neighborhood, Mick's house had a 6 foot wooden privacy fence that enclosed the back yard. Even if they were trying to keep an eye on his back yard from their vehicle, Mick realized that they wouldn't be able to see him through the fence, and he knew that the only way that he had a chance to escape was through the back.

Mick went back to the front door to check one last time that the Marshals were still in their vehicle, which they were. He pulled his favorite old Cleveland Indians baseball cap down over his eyes, put on a pair of sunglasses, and swiftly moved towards the back door of his house.

He cautiously opened the back door to his house just wide enough so that he could slip through, gently closed the door behind him, and walked as fast as he could in a crouching position towards the detached garage that was situated on the back of his property.

Once Mick had made it to the four foot gap between the back of his garage and the privacy fence, he leaned against the back wall to catch his breath and make sure that he didn't hear the sounds of anyone trying to approach. Convinced he was still in the clear, Mick looked at the two damaged planks along the fence line, that despite being broken for years, he had never gotten around to fixing.

For once, Mick's procrastination had paid off and he began to pull on the rotted wood as quietly as he could in an effort to give himself an exit strategy. The first plank almost disintegrated in his hands and he managed to remove it from the fence rails that ran horizontally and perpendicular to the posts. After gently placing what remained of the plank on the ground, Mick peered around the corner of the garage to make sure that he was still alone and was relieved to discover that he was.

The second plank proved to be a little more challenging to remove because the nails had become rusted into the wood. After a few minutes of cautiously shifting the plank back and forth, Mick was finally able to remove the plank and set it on the ground.

*Late Life*

He peered through the fence and surveyed his neighbor's yard to the back, which was enclosed with a four foot chain link fence, and determined that it was clear. Mick knew the young married couple that lived there well enough to know that they both worked during the day, the man a first shift assembly line worker at the Ford plant and his wife a bank teller, so he didn't anticipate running into either of them when he finally made his break for it.

Mick took one last look around the corner of his garage, breathed a sigh of relief that he was still alone, and decided to make his move. After squeezing through the exposed rails in the narrow gap that he had created in the fence, Mick briskly walked toward the driveway gate in his neighbor's chain link fence.

Before he opened the gate, Mick did his best to scan the street in front of their house to see if there was another SUV keeping an eye on the area. After determining that the area was clear, he quickly exited through the gate and tried to walk as nonchalantly down the sidewalk away from the house as possible.

Mick's heart raced as he simultaneously tried to put as much distance between him and his house as possible while also making sure that he wasn't being followed. Once he reached the first intersection, Mick crossed the street and headed northbound away from his house.

While his feet had taken him this far, Mick knew that he would need a car if he was ever going to make it out of the city. While he had no idea where he would go once he had a vehicle, he did know the best way to find a set of wheels.

*Late Life*

# 47

Cooper Madison sat inside Oakland International Airport's private jet suite as he waited to board his chartered flight, courtesy of Todd Taylor, back home to Cleveland. He had unsuccessfully attempted to call Cara numerous times throughout the morning in an effort to help her understand what really happened the previous evening at the Uptown Nightclub. Frustrated, he decided to give Clarence a call.

"Hey, Clarence," Coop began when his bodyguard and occasional life coach answered. "I know T gave you a call already, but I just wanted to make sure you knew when to get me from the airport when I land."

"Yessir," Clarence confirmed. "We're all set. I'll meet you on the tarmac at Burke Lakefront when you land. How are you feeling this morning? It's pretty early there still, isn't it?"

"I'm moving like a herd of turtles, Clarence. It's been a rough start to the day," Coop replied.

"That's what I've been told," Clarence acknowledged. "You hanging in there?"

"I suppose..."

"Have you spoken to Cara yet?"

"Not since she hung up on me this morning," Coop sighed.

"This, too, shall pass, Coop," said Clarence. "She just needs some time to process everything. She'll come around."

"I know," Coop agreed. "I just wish I could talk to her. She won't answer any of my calls. I don't even know where she is..."

"Apparently, she and Lucy went on a little road trip to Columbus to go shopping. If Cara is anything like my wife, when she needs some retail therapy, you better prepare yourself for that credit card bill," Clarence chuckled, despite knowing that money would never be an issue for Coop.

"It'll be worth it if it calms her down a little," Coop affirmed. "How'd you find out that she was going to Columbus?"

"Jason gave me a call. Apparently Cara left her phone back in Cleveland and used Lucy's to leave a message for him at work," informed Clarence. "I guess Cara was supposed to take Gabby to the zoo today, but she obviously had a change in plans. Jason seemed like he was pretty busy when I spoke to him, so I wasn't able to get much more from him."

The news of Cara's cancellation of the planned trip with her niece didn't do anything to make Coop feel better about the situation. She loved Gabby as much as any aunt could, so for her to bail on her meant that Cara was truly in a bad place. Coop couldn't blame her.

"Is she coming back to Cleveland later?" Coop asked, hoping that he'd be able to see her in person once he was back in Cleveland. If not, he had already made up his mind that he would travel to Columbus to find her.

"As far as I know this is just a day trip," Clarence said in response.

Coop sighed, "Man, I feel like I've been chewed up and spit out. In the matter of one evening I went from being on top of the world to feeling like ten miles of bad road."

"That was one heck of a game you pitched last night," Clarence said, hoping to shift Coop's focus to the positive.

"Thanks, Clarence," Coop replied, a smile forming on his face for the first time all morning as he recalled his perfect game heroics. "I was in the zone, wasn't I?"

"Boy, you were on fire!" Clarence bellowed, pleased that he detected a small change in Coop's demeanor.

"I don't know if I'll ever pitch like that again," Coop admitted. "I can't explain it. It was as if every pitch that CD called was exactly what my arm wanted to throw."

"What do athletes call that again? Being in the zone?" Clarence asked.

"Yessir," Coop agreed. "I've been in that zone a few times in my career, but nothing like that. If I could bottle that feeling up, I'd have somethin' sweeter than Yoo-Hoo."

The last sentence Coop said brought out a loud laugh from Clarence, who genuinely had grown to love the young man that he was entrusted to protect. He knew that Coop looked to him for fatherly advice, and he was always happy to oblige.

After the call had ended, Clarence felt a little melancholy as he thought about the secret that he had been keeping from Coop, and he hoped that the ballplayer would understand once he became aware.

*Late Life*

# 48

Detective Jason Knox, who was accompanied by Brad Coreno and the two other United States Marshals that had been doing surveillance on Mick's house, knocked on the front door of his commander's west side bungalow.

He had tried calling Mick before he arrived, per Brad's plan, but did not get an answer. Jason had hoped that it just meant that Mick was asleep, but his gut told him otherwise.

After a few minutes of knocking on the door with no response, Brad said to the other two Marshals, "You two stay here while Detective Knox and I go to the back of the house and see if we can't peek inside. You guys are positive that he didn't leave the house this morning, right?"

His partners both replied that they had not seen any movement on the house since arriving earlier that morning. One of them wondered if Mick had even been home at all, to which Jason informed Brad could have been a real possibility since Mick was known to sometimes go home from the bar with whatever female companion he could find.

"I'll see if it's unlocked," Jason had said to Brad as they approached the back door, which after a wiggle of the handle proved to be locked shut.

"I don't see any signs of life inside either," Brad replied as he peered through the door's glass window.

"What now?" Jason asked.

"Well, we have a team on standby to breach his house and perform the search warrant," Brad informed. "I'll give them a call after we take a look around the property. I realized as we approached the backyard that he could've possibly gone out the back door undetected. This fence is pretty high."

"I'm guessing that you didn't have anyone watching that street," Jason said as he nodded towards the house that butted up against Mick's back yard.

"Usually we would, with a little more notice," Brad conceded. "But, we had to work with what we had this morning after Mick didn't show up at the precinct."

Jason nodded in agreement, as he could relate. He also knew that hindsight was 20/20 in situations like this. There had been many times throughout his career as an officer when he chose to go into a situation shorthanded due to time constraints or a lack of resources.

As the pair made their way to the back of the garage, they both stopped in unison when they realized that there was an opening in the fence.

"Shit!" Brad exclaimed as he sprinted towards the gap which had two rotted and broken wooden planks on the ground beside it.

Jason followed suit and they both peered through the opening to see if there was any sign of Mick. There wasn't.

Brad yelled for the two Marshals standing guard at the front door and retrieved his cell phone from his pocket. He held the index finger up on his other hand to tell Jason to wait while he made the call.

"Yeah, this is Coreno," he spoke into the phone. "Send the team over now to breach the house. Suspect is likely on the run. We'll wait here until you arrive."

As soon as the call was over, Jason asked, "You want me to call it in to our department?"

"Yes," Brad confirmed. "He's obviously on foot, so even if he got spooked and bolted early this morning when my guys first arrived, he likely couldn't have gotten that far."

Jason used his cell phone to call Chief of Police Anthony Lawson, not only to fill him in on the entire situation, but also in hopes that he would know the best way to put out an APB on one of their own.

Chief Lawson, though every bit as shocked as Jason and also equally as upset that he didn't know about any of this prior to Jason's call, reassured the detective that he would have every police car in the area looking for Mick within minutes.

"Detective Knox," Chief Lawson interjected just as Jason was about to end the call. "Do you really think Commander McCarthy is capable of doing any of this?"

"I don't know what to think anymore, Chief," Jason admitted. "What I will say is that it definitely was Mick in those images that the Marshals showed me this morning. Whether he did what they said he did, or not, we need to find him as soon as possible so that if he is innocent, he can give his side of the story."

The Chief of Police, who had taken over control of the department after HoJo's death, concurred and ordered Jason to keep him posted on anything and everything from that point forward. He added that he would be on his way to Mick's house as soon as he handled putting out the APB on Mick before hanging up.

A little over ten miles away, Mick drove the sedan that he had commandeered a few blocks from his house. He had nearly made the elderly woman pass out from shock when he approached her car at a stop sign, flashed his badge, and screamed that he needed her car for official police business. The terrified woman complied and watched in disbelief as Mick sped away in her car, leaving her standing alone and crying in the middle of the intersection.

*Late Life*

Mick was safely outside Cleveland's city limits as he headed southbound on Interstate 71 in the direction of Strongsville's South Park Mall. Once at the mall, Mick planned to abandon the car in the vast parking lot that encompassed the entire shopping complex and then figure out his next move.

As he exited the freeway via the Route 82 exit near the mall, Mick began to cycle through the limited choices that he would have in order to escape. He was well aware that being a fugitive of the U.S. Marshal Service meant that there was no such thing as a "safe" place for him to be as long as he was still in the country, and while leaving the country would be his best bet, that also presented a huge array of complications.

Whatever path he chose, Mick was only certain of one thing: that he wouldn't go down without a fight.

# 49

Cara and Lucy giggled as they recounted their successful day of retail therapy in Columbus. It had been a short, yet very expensive trip, thanks to the extremely exclusive American Express "Black Card" that Cara had used to pay for their haul.

The credit card, which was only available to the wealthiest of clients, had become a status symbol for those lucky enough to have one. A few months earlier, Coop had added Cara to his account and given her the card with her name on it.

She had rarely used the card since obtaining it, mostly because she felt guilty that she still had yet to get a "real" job after graduating from Cleveland State University with a Bachelor's Degree in Business and Economics. She had worked hard to help put herself through school, and it was while she was delivering food for Stucky's Place that she had met Coop, but their relationship had made it difficult for her to find a job where she wouldn't constantly have to fight the stigma of being Cooper Madison's girlfriend.

It's not that Cara wasn't putting her degree to use. Coop, with the help of his agent Todd Taylor's finance division at IMG, had put Cara in charge of managing his day-to-day finances. She had even received a small salary from IMG, the sports agency started in 1960 in Cleveland by its visionary founder, Mark McCormack. While it was a job that Cara took very seriously, she also felt as if she hadn't earned it.

"Oh my God, Cara," Lucy laughed as she recounted, "When you pulled that Black Card out at the Coach store, I thought that the salesgirl's jaw was going to hit the floor!"

"For sure!" Cara agreed. "You know she looked at us when we put all those purses and bags on the counter that there was no way we could actually afford to pay for them."

"But then... BAM! Amex Black Card!" Lucy shouted as she smacked the steering wheel of her car for emphasis.

"The ultimate 'mic drop'!" Cara added as she pantomimed dropping an imaginary microphone.

"Make sure you thank Coop for me, by the way. I absolutely *adore* the purse he doesn't realize that he bought me," Lucy laughed.

While her words were meant in jest, they nonetheless stirred up the feelings of sadness and anger that Cara had been trying to suppress throughout the day. While she had hoped that the shopping trip would help her forget the CMZ article, it had only proved to be a temporary distraction as the emotions were still too fresh.

Lucy, realizing that she probably shouldn't have brought up Coop's name, said, "I'm sorry, Carebear…"

"Don't be," Cara reassured her best friend with a forced smile.

"Are you going to call him later?" Lucy asked as she merged her car northbound onto Interstate 71 towards Cleveland.

Cara sighed, "I don't know if I'm ready for that, yet…"

"I get it," Lucy replied.

"I mean, I know deep in my heart that it probably wasn't his fault," Cara admitted. "I guess I'm just pissed off that he was naive enough to pose for a picture with those two sluts. Not to mention that the picture is there for the entire world to see on the internet."

"CMZ has done you guys dirty so much since you've been together," Lucy pointed out. "The Gary Boardman pictures alone were bad enough..."

The mere mention of Gary Boardman's name made Cara's skin crawl. The paparazzo had not only been responsible for first leaking pictures of the couple at the beginning of their relationship to the gossip website, but he had also followed them to Florida following Coop's Tommy John surgery.

It was in Florida that the photographer managed to snap pictures of a topless Cara as she and Coop sunbathed, where they had assumed that they were alone on Todd Taylor's private property. He subsequently sold the salacious shots to CMZ who immediately ran a story with the topless, albeit censored, pictures of Cara.

Thanks to the quick thinking and tremendous clout of Todd Taylor, the story was taken down not long after it was posted, and Gary Boardman was arrested on trespassing and voyeurism charges. Cara found some satisfaction, albeit at her expense, that the topless photos of her were what led to the authorities' discovery of thousands of incriminating images on the paparazzo's computer.

Many of the photos found on his hard drive contained explicit images of underage girls as they unknowingly were photographed via a telescopic lens by the creepy cameraman. While Cara was relieved to know that Gary Boardman would be in prison for the foreseeable future, the past night's CMZ story was a cruel reminder that living in the public eye was always going to be a challenge.

Cara thought of that as she and Lucy drove back towards Cleveland, and she began to feel a tinge of empathy for Coop. While she was, and would remain, angry that their personal lives had once again been infringed upon by the gossip website, she also knew that Coop loved her enough that he never would've purposely meant for that to happen.

Her thoughts were interrupted when Lucy asked, "So where are we going once we're back in Cleveland? Do you want me to stop at the Westcott so you can get your phone and some clothes?"

Cara weighed their options before responding, "You know what? I really just want to see my mom. I feel bad that she probably has seen the CMZ story and has probably tried to call me, too. She's got to be worried about me, so let's go straight to her house."

"To Brook Park we shall go!" Lucy declared as if she was a Civil War general leading troops into battle.

Cara laughed at the sight of her best friend, who continued the charade by pretending to play a bugle, and felt grateful to have Lucy Eckert in her life. They had been through so much together over the years, from first loves to first heartbreaks, and had always had each other's backs.

As Lucy's car headed northbound, what had been an unseasonably warm and sunny early autumn day began to show signs that an impending storm was beginning to brew in the distance.

# 50

Detective Jason Knox had been driving all over Cleveland in the hours since Mick's house was raided by the United States Marshal Service's Fugitive Task Force. The search of Mick's house had not turned up anything incriminating, initially, but the computer taken from the scene still had to be examined by forensic specialists.

Knowing Mick and his disdain for technology in general, Jason believed that the impending search of the computer would be an exercise in futility, as he was pretty certain that Mick likely only used it to play solitaire.

After staying at his commander's house for the duration of the search, he and Marshal Brad Coreno had decided to hop in Jason's unmarked police cruiser and canvas the area for any signs of Mick, to no avail.

"I think that we should go to Zoey's apartment," Jason said after circling Mick's neighborhood for what he figured had to be the tenth time.

"Is that the ex-wife?" Brad asked.

"Yeah, she lives with her new husband in a luxury waterfront condo in Lakewood not too far from here," Jason replied.

"Sounds like she upgraded," Brad mused.

"You could say that," Jason agreed. "Her new husband is some bigshot HR guy pulling in six figures. According to Mick, all Zoey does these days is enjoy the fruits of his labor."

"Do you think he might've gone there?" Brad inquired. "Maybe Mick decided to pay his ex a revenge visit before getting out of the city…"

"Do I think that he would want to? Yes," Jason confirmed before adding, "But, I also don't think that he'd be dumb enough to risk it. Mick's a really smart guy, despite his issues. You don't get promoted to commander by being an idiot."

"Agreed," Brad replied. "At the very least we can see if maybe he has contacted her, and we can warn her that Mick's on the run."

Fifteen minutes later, Jason and Brad approached the front entrance to Zoey's condominium building. The Carlyle on the Lake condominium complex was located in what was known as the "Gold Coast" community along the banks of Lake Erie on Edgewater Drive.

The prestigious waterfront neighborhood had been a desirable place for Cleveland's most successful clientele to call home ever since the early 1970's when the area had been fully developed. The Carlyle, built in 1969, had been one of the first complexes on the Gold Coast to provide its wealthy inhabitants both a breathtaking view of the lake and a short commute to the city, where many of them worked.

"Here goes nothing," Jason said as he pressed the call button next to the name "Hellickson" on the building's multi-tenant intercom system.

"Hello?" a woman's voice came through the small speaker located alongside the rows of buttons.

"Zoey," Jason said, clearing his throat. "It's Jason. I was hoping that I could come up and talk with you for a minute if that's okay?"

"Jason Knox?" Zoey asked in a surprised tone.

Jason had always liked Zoey, and while he obviously didn't approve of her extramarital affair, he would be lying if he said that he didn't understand why she had left Mick. She had never been anything but nice to him, as well, but he also hadn't spoken to her since before the divorce.

"The one and only," Jason replied awkwardly, hoping that there was still enough goodwill between the two of them that she would let them up.

"Is everything okay?" a puzzled Zoey inquired.

"Well, that's what we wanted to come up and speak to you about," Jason answered.

"We?" Zoey pressed.

"Oh, yeah," Jason said, realizing that he hadn't mentioned Brad. "I also have Brad Coreno from the United States Marshal Service here with me. Listen, I promise I'll explain everything once we're up."

There was no response from Zoey; however, a few seconds later a buzzer sounded and along with it came the distinct click of the entry door being automatically unlocked. A relieved Jason shrugged as he flashed a smile at Brad, who had already reached to open the door.

Zoey, who had been waiting for the pair at the entrance of her condo as they exited the elevator on the 20th floor, stood with her arms crossed and wore a worried expression on her face. The petite brunette had never looked better, Jason thought to himself upon seeing her, and had obviously been taking full advantage of the workout facility that the Carlyle offered.

"Hi, Zoey," Jason said before turning to introduce the man standing next to him. "This is Marshal Brad Coreno."

"Hello, ma'am," Brad followed up, flashing his credentials. "We appreciate you taking the time to see us, albeit it unannounced."

Zoey decided to skip past any pleasantries and asked, "What the hell is this all about, Jason?"

Before Jason could respond, Brad interjected, "It would be best if we discussed this inside, ma'am."

Zoey reluctantly invited the men inside her condo, which was every bit as luxurious and modern as Jason had imagined it would be. The windows that adorned the far wall of the unit offered a spectacular view of Lake Erie, and the early afternoon sun had provided all the illumination that the room needed. Zoey stood just a few steps inside the condo after closing the door behind them, her body language made it clear that she was not about to offer the men a seat inside.

"Okay, you're inside," Zoey said sharply before demanding, "now tell me what the hell is going on…"

"It's Mick…" Jason began.

"Is he dead?" Zoey asked before Jason could finish his sentence, though by her tone Jason couldn't tell which answer she was hoping to get in return.

"No, he's not dead," Jason replied. "But, he is in some trouble. Have you heard from him at all recently?"

"What kind of trouble?" she countered, before adding, "but, no, I haven't heard from that asshole in months."

"We aren't at liberty to discuss the specifics of the case, ma'am," Brad stepped in, "but, what we can tell you is that Mick is currently being considered a fugitive in a murder case."

"*Murder* case?" a very bewildered Zoey asked before looking to Jason. "Is this guy for real?"

"I'm afraid so, Zoey," Jason confirmed.

314

"Okay, hold on a second," Zoey said as she brought both hands up to her forehead as if to use them to help her process the news. "Let me get this straight... Mick is wanted for a *murder*? And he's on the *run*?"

Jason simply nodded in the affirmative, knowing exactly how she felt. He had felt the same the entire day, as well.

"Do you happen to know where Mick might have gone today?" Brad asked, before adding, "I mean, throughout your time as his wife was there any place, perhaps a relative's house, that Mick would ever go to if he wanted to get away for awhile?"

"The only place Mick ever seemed to go was the bar," Zoey answered, forcing a laugh. "He didn't have any real friends outside of the force. Hell, he would even go to Las Vegas by himself to gamble. I asked him once if I could tag along and he laughed in my face. God, marrying him was the worst decision I ever made!"

Jason, who had anticipated that Zoey likely wouldn't have any insight on where Mick was, did want to make sure that she understood the severity of the situation without divulging too many details.

"Zoey, you probably don't have anything to worry about," Jason said, "but, I would definitely give your husband a call and let him know the situation. I'm going to make sure that Lakewood Police keeps an eye on your condo building, but I would still be cautious in regards to letting anyone up if they try to buzz you."

"Oh my God! Hunter!" Zoey gasped in reference to her husband. "He's at his office downtown. You don't think Mick would go there, do you?"

"It's highly unlikely that Mick would visibly put himself anywhere in Cleveland right now, ma'am," Brad replied. "My guess is that he is either laying low somewhere within the city or has managed to get as far away as possible."

"That being said," Jason added. "I can send a patrol car to his office just to be safe. They can follow him all the way back here to your condo. I would just try and sit tight here until we find Mick."

"When do you think that will be?" Zoey asked, who looked more and more worried as the gravity of the situation began to take effect.

"Hopefully, very soon," Jason responded.

It wasn't the amount of time that it would take to find Mick that Jason worried about the most; it was what would happen when they did.

*Late Life*

# 51

"You sure that you don't want to come in?" Coop asked Clarence before exiting his bodyguard's SUV, which had just parked on the street in front of Joanne Knox's split level house in Brook Park.

Clarence, who had picked Coop up after his chartered jet landed at Cleveland's Burke Lakefront Airport, had received a call from Cara earlier informing him that she had planned to stay at her mom's house that evening.

It was Joanne who had insisted that Cara give Clarence a call. Earlier that day, Clarence had phoned the recently widowed Joanne to see if she had heard from her daughter. While Joanne hadn't heard from Cara, she made Clarence a promise that she would contact him as soon as she did.

"No, I'm good," Clarence replied. "I'll be out here if you need me."

Coop thanked him for the lift and cautiously approached the front door of Cara's childhood home. He wasn't sure how she would react to his visit, especially since he had told Clarence not to tell anyone that he was coming back to town.

At the time, Coop was certain that a surprise visit would be the best approach to smooth things over with Cara. However, as he nervously took a deep breath before knocking on the door, he began to second guess his decision.

"I'll get it!" he heard Cara's voice come from inside the house, followed by footsteps as she bounded down the short flight of steps towards the front door.

"Hey, girl," Coop said after a bewildered Cara opened the door and realized that her boyfriend, whom she had fully expected to be sitting somewhere in Oakland's visiting clubhouse with the rest of his teammates as they prepared for that evening's game, stood before her.

"What on Earth are you doing here?" Cara asked, a puzzled look on her face.

"Well, you see, it's kind of a funny story," Coop spoke the lines that he had rehearsed over and over in his head during his flight home. "Last night, something really crazy happened, and while I certainly didn't mean for it to hurt you, I know it did. I guess I just figured that an apology was best given in person, so… here I am…"

While Coop may have had the length of a cross-country flight to figure out what he would say to Cara, she found herself totally unprepared to respond. She had spent most of the day imagining herself giving Coop a tongue-lashing of epic proportions before she would even begin to allow herself to look vulnerable in front of him, yet she found herself being just that as she stared at those steely blue eyes of his that had always given him an unfair advantage in moments like this.

"I don't understand…" Cara began, before adding, "Aren't you supposed to be with the team?"

"Yeah, I am," Coop replied. He took a step closer to Cara, lowered his voice and said, "But, I told them that I had somewhere far more important to be…"

321

Cara wanted to yell at him for putting her through yet another public shaming courtesy of CMZ, but when she opened her mouth to speak the only words that came out were, "I love you…"

"I love you more," Coop said with conviction as he pulled her close, enveloping her athletic body inside his hulking frame. "I'm so sorry, Cara…"

Cara, who by now had tears streaming down her cheeks, felt her entire body give itself to his. She melted in his arms as he kissed the top of her head, which was firmly planted on his broad, muscular chest. The two lovers remained in that embrace, the rest of the world around them a blur, for the next few minutes.

It was Cara who finally broke the silence.

"I don't know if I'll ever be strong enough to deal with this stuff, Coop…"

"Don't you realize," he said, gently lifting her chin up with his massive hand so that he could look her in the eyes, "you already *are* that strong. Look at everything we've already been through, Cara. You're the strongest girl I know…"

322

Cara could see that it was Coop who now had tears in his eyes, which only made her even more emotional as she leaned in for a kiss that made her entire body shudder with passion.

Clarence, who had been watching the entire interaction unfold from the front seat of his Escalade, which was still running as he listened to the radio, felt a wave of satisfaction come over him as the young couple kissed. While he knew that relationships, especially ones involving a famous professional athlete, were hard to maintain in the long-term, he had always believed that if anyone could make it, it would be Coop and Cara.

Witnessing two people in love come together, and knowing that he had played a small part in it, made Clarence extremely grateful that he had been lucky enough to be there in that moment. He smiled as he watched the pair enter Joanne's house, hand in hand.

Being so wrapped up in the moment was perhaps the reason that Clarence, who rarely ever let his guard down while "on duty", didn't notice the figure as it approached the passenger side of his vehicle from the rear.

By the time the rear door was flung open, it was too late for Clarence to do anything about the gun pointed at his head.

*Late Life*

# 52

At first, Mick was as surprised as anyone when Clarence's SUV pulled in front of the Knox residence and he observed Coop get out. He had no idea why the pitcher, whom he had just witnessed throw a perfect game on television in Oakland the night before, was back in Cleveland.

It was the second surprise that evening, as Mick had assumed that Joanne would be all alone in her house. However, when he saw Cara's friend pull into the driveway and drop her off, he had almost abandoned his plan to leave the country via the Canadian border entrance in Windsor, Ontario.

Mick, ever the opportunist, soon realized that despite the presence of the two very large males, that his plan had actually improved its chances of succeeding. He truly believed that Lady Luck seemed to be on his side. So far, that luck had helped him escape his house undetected and had even led him to the vehicle that he had driven to Joanne's house.

Earlier that day, Mick had hopped on an RTA bus at one of the stops along Route 82 by the mall, where he had abandoned the sedan that he had commandeered from the elderly woman that morning. Knowing that he would need a car, but also knowing that attempting to steal one would be too risky, Mick decided to keep his eyes peeled for something cheap that he could buy with the cash he had in his bugout bag.

Mick figured that his best bet would be one of the many cars with a "For Sale by Owner" sign that were often found sitting in front yards. He had passed many of them without giving them a second thought over the years, but he now realized that finding one could be his ticket to freedom.

When the bus that he was on made a stop near the intersection of Pearl Road and Meadow Lane in Strongsville, Mick made the decision to get off and walk through the nearby neighborhood.

He didn't have to walk far down Meadow Lane before he found an older model Chevy S-10 pickup for sale in front of one of the many modest homes along that street. The small, four cylinder truck, which he guessed was at least 15 years old, had almost as much rust as it did faded red paint. The handwritten "For Sale" sign indicated that the truck was a 1982 model year, and that the seller was looking for $900 or best offer.

"Are ya interested?" a male voice shouted from inside the house's garage.

Mick turned to see an older man, who appeared to be in his 70's, approach the truck as he wiped his hands with a shop towel.

"Well, that depends," Mick replied, turning on the charm. "Does it run?"

"Runs better than it looks, that's for sure," the man laughed.

"Well, that's a relief," Mick chuckled.

"Yeah, I bought it used about ten years ago to use as a work truck. I'm a retired plumber, but I don't have much use for it anymore since I splurged on that," the man said as he nodded towards the brand new Chevy Silverado that sat in his driveway.

Mick whistled and said, "That sure is a beauty of truck, mister. I can see why you don't need this old girl anymore."

"I figured I'd earned the right to treat myself to something nicer," the man said proudly. "Life's too short not to live a little, right?"

"You can say that again!" Mick agreed enthusiastically.

"I will tell you, though," the man said as he gestured towards the S-10, "This old thing may have a lot of miles on it, almost 200,000 to be exact, but it'll start right up for you every time."

"To be honest, that's all I really need it for," Mick replied. "I've been looking for a work truck like this for awhile now."

"What kind of work do you do?" the man asked.

"I paint houses," Mick lied.

"Oh yeah?" the old timer responded. "You'll have to give me your card. I've been meaning to put a fresh coat on the house for some time."

"I would if I had any on me," Mick said. "To be honest, my daily driver is down the street at the dealer's repair shop getting new brakes put on, so I figured I'd kill some time by going for a walk, and luckily for me, I came across this truck."

"Oh, you mean over there at Pete Baur Pontiac?" the man asked, referring to the longtime Strongsville car dealership.

"That's the one," Mick confirmed. "I got me a 2002 Grand Prix from there, but it's getting to that age where I'm starting to really have to put some money in it. Last month it was the alternator, this month it's the brakes."

"Isn't that the way it always is?" the man mused. "You pay finally the damn thing off just in time for everything to start going bad."

"Tell me about it!" Mick laughed. "I'm gonna have to start painting twice the number of houses just to pay for all the damn repairs."

"So, do you want to take her for a spin?" the man asked.

"To be honest, I don't really have a lot of time," Mick replied. "I figure if I buy it I'll only have an hour or so to get it over to the license bureau for new tags and still have time to get my Grand Prix back from the dealer. How about I make you an offer right now, in cash, and I'll take this old girl off your hands? You don't seem like a guy who would be anything but honest with me, so as long as it starts up and drives, we'll have a deal."

Surprised, the man asked, "You have that much cash on you?"

"Well, I had stopped at the bank to take out enough cash to pay for the brakes, so I have that on me," Mick replied. "I always pay in cash, if possible, because the dealer will sometimes knock a few bucks off the price."

"Nothing wrong with that," the man agreed. "What kind of offer are ya thinkin'?"

"Well, I'm not trying to low-ball ya," Mick said, "but I only have enough cash on me to offer you $600."

The man thought the offer over for a few seconds, and then replied, "I'll tell you what... I'll accept your offer of $600 today, as long as you promise to swing by here sometime this week and give me an estimate to paint my house. If you're willing to knock a hundred bucks off what you would normally charge for the job, then you have yourself a deal."

"That works for me," Mick said as he shook the man's hand. "I'll even knock $200 off the cost of the job, as a thank you."

"Even better!" the man agreed. "I'll go inside and get the title and keys. I hope you don't need me to go to the license bureau with you. I'm in the middle of fixing my lawnmower. I hope it's okay if I just sign the title over to you and let you take it from there."

"That would be just fine by me," Mick replied.

"I'm sorry, I never did ask you your name," the man said, slightly embarrassed.

"It's Eugene," Mick answered. "Eugene Lankford…"

"Hmmm, that name sounds familiar to me for some reason," the man said.

"I get that all the time," Mick chuckled. "I'm not sure why either. What's your name?"

"Lou Roman," the man said. "Listen, I won't keep you any longer. I'll go grab that title and both sets of keys for ya so you can be on your way."

"Good deal, Lou," Mick called out as he watched the old man shuffle towards his house.

An hour later, as Mick sat inside his recently purchased truck in the parking lot of Strongsville's Wal-Mart, he hatched the plan that had initially led him to Joanne Knox's house. While he was well aware that going to Joanne's house was going to be risky, he also knew that he didn't have many options left if he was going to make it to Canada.

*Late Life*

# 53

"Put your hands on the wheel," Mick ordered in a hushed tone from the back seat as he briefly glanced at the front door to Joanne's house to make sure that Coop and Cara had not witnessed his ambush.

"Mick?" a shocked Clarence responded. "What the hell are you doing?"

"Put your goddamn hands on the wheel, Clarence!" Mick reiterated as he moved to the seat directly behind Clarence so that his gun was pointed at the back of the driver's head.

Clarence reluctantly obliged as he tried his best to assess the situation. He had hoped that whatever it was that Mick was trying to do would involve him having Clarence take him far away from Joanne's house, where inside the people that he was sworn to protect currently were.

Unbeknownst to Clarence, that was exactly what Mick had in mind, too. It wasn't his initial plan, which had been to kidnap Joanne and force her to drive him to Windsor. Since Joanne did still own the wheelchair accessible van that her paraplegic husband had used to get around town, Mick had hoped that riding in that would increase their chances of making it into Canada.

While he and the late Charlie Knox weren't exactly doppelgängers, let alone close to being the same age, Mick figured that if he pulled his baseball cap down over his eyes and pretended to sleep his way across the border, that it just might work. If it didn't, they would simply turn the van around and he would leave Joanne behind somewhere in Detroit while he came up with another plan.

Mick's entire plan was based on the assumption that Joanne still had Charlie's driver's license and birth certificate, which he was certain that she likely hadn't gotten rid of in the weeks since his death. Since no passport was required to enter Canada from the U.S., providing that the traveler had a government-issued ID and birth certificate, Mick felt confident that they would be able to cross the border without any major issues.

Mick had crossed into Ontario via Detroit at least half a dozen times over the years to gamble at Casino Windsor, and the lax border security would often barely look at his passport before letting him through. Reentering the U.S. was an entirely different experience, especially since 9/11, but Mick had no plans of doing that any time soon.

All of that planning was thrown out the window, however, once Mick had realized that Cara and Coop were there with Joanne. Kidnapping Joanne would have been tough to pull off by itself, but abducting two women was far too risky. While kidnapping a former cop and a professional baseball player wasn't exactly a sane plan either, the quick-thinking Mick believed that it was as good as it would get for him.

As he had waited for Coop and Cara to go inside the house after their passionate reunion on the front steps of Joanne's house, Mick decided that the best way to get out of the country would be by forcing Coop and his bodyguard to drive him to an ATM and have the wealthy ballplayer take out as much cash as his bank would allow. He would then force Coop and Clarence out of the SUV somewhere in the middle of nowhere, leaving them without as much as a cell phone, and use their vehicle to drive as far away as he could until he could ditch it and work on another scheme.

Mick knew that any plan for him to evade capture would be a marathon and not a sprint, and his initial Windsor plan was far too much of a sprint to guarantee success. He was in this for the long haul, even if it meant hitchhiking across the country after abandoning Clarence's SUV. As long as he had his gun, badge, and some extra cash, Mick was confident that he would find a way to maintain his freedom. Prison was no place for a former cop to be, and Mick had made himself a promise that he would never let himself be put in that situation.

"Mick, just what the hell is going on?" Clarence pleaded for a response as Mick continued to aim his Glock at him from the back seat of his SUV.

"No more questions, Clarence," warned Mick. "Just do as I tell you and nobody will get hurt."

Clarence remained silent, his hands on the steering wheel, as Mick had instructed him.

"What you're going to do first is slowly, and I mean slowly, remove the gun that I know you have on you and hand it to me," Mick ordered.

Clarence slowly reached inside of the black sport coat that he was wearing and cautiously withdrew his gun from its holster and held it, barrel pointed downward, over his right shoulder for Mick to grab.

"Good," Mick said, taking the gun and placing it on the seat next to him. "Now, I want you to listen very carefully… You're going to call Coop on his cell phone and tell him that you need him to come out to the vehicle, alone. Don't even think about trying to warn him, or I'll put a bullet in your head and then go do the same to everyone in that house, you understand?"

"I understand," Clarence replied, trying to remain as calm as possible and make Mick feel as though he was in charge. "But, Mick, what if he asks why I need him to come out?"

"You're a smart man, Clarence," Mick chuckled coldly. "You'll figure something out. If not, well, you know what'll happen…"

Clarence took a deep breath and reached for his phone, which was mounted on his windshield by a suction cup holder; but before he could grab it, he heard the front door of the Knox house open and saw Coop and Cara exit and head in their direction.

"Shit!" Mick hissed as he, too, witnessed the young couple approaching.

"Hey, Clarence!" Coop called out. "Come on inside, man. We have pizza coming."

"You better come in and join us, Clarence!" Cara warned, playfully.

Clarence felt his heart sink as the couple continued to approach the vehicle, wishing that there was a way that he could get them to stop before it was too late.

"Pick the phone up and pretend to talk on it," Mick whispered from the back seat.

Clarence quickly snatched the phone off the windshield and held it up to his ear and pretended as if he was listening intently to someone on the other end of the call. He had hoped that the darkness of the early evening, along with his Escalade's tinted windows, would prevent them from seeing Mick in the back seat as they continued to get closer.

"Now, roll your window down halfway and tell them you're on a call and that you'll be in soon," Mick ordered. "And don't try to pull any shit…"

Clarence rolled his driver's side window down halfway as instructed and began gesturing to Coop and Cara that he was on a call. He pretended to cover the microphone on his cell phone and whispered, "I'll be in shortly…"

Before Coop or Cara could answer, Clarence's phone began to ring loudly in his hand. The call flustered the normally calm and collected bodyguard and he began to fumble with the still-ringing phone as he tried to stop it from ringing.

Coop and Cara, who by this point were just a few steps from the Escalade, seemed to be as equally caught off guard as their bodyguard was by the sound of the ringtone. Clarence, who had finally managed to silence his phone, seemed at a loss for words as he just stared at them and smiled.

"Is everything alright, Clarence?" a concerned Coop asked.

Cara, sensing something definitely was peculiar, decided to approach the driver's side window even closer. Before Clarence could say anything, he heard the sound of his rear passenger window going down.

"Get in," Mick ordered the couple in a disturbingly calm manner.

"Mick?" Cara asked, completely shocked seeing her older brother's boss in the back seat as well as hearing the words coming from his mouth.

"I said, get in," Mick bristled through clenched teeth, only this time he made sure that the pair saw his gun.

The sight of the gun caused Coop to immediately step between Cara and the SUV before saying, "What's goin' on here, fellas?"

"Just do as I say and nobody will get hurt," Mick seethed.

"Clarence, what the hell is going on?" Cara pleaded, still trying to process the situation, as Coop continued to shield her from Mick.

"Hey kids, come inside!" the voice of a concerned Joanne Knox called out from the front door of her house. "I just got a phone call from Jason. He said to make sure that everyone was in the house and to lock the doors. You guys won't believe what he just told me about Mick!"

The words had just left Joanne's mouth when she took a closer look at Clarence's SUV. She felt a shiver of panic when she saw the man that her son had just called to warn her about seated in the back seat, his face illuminated by the glow of the street lamp.

Joanne, who had instantly become nearly frozen with fear, watched in horror as she witnessed Mick aim what appeared to be a gun in the direction of her daughter and Coop. As the realization hit her that she may have just made a bad situation worse by coming outside, Joanne closed her eyes and said a silent prayer.

*Late Life*

# 54

Grace Brooks had driven as quickly as she could to Joanne's house after receiving a troubling call from Jason. At that time, she had been waiting to pick up the order that Cara had placed earlier at Kicker's Pizza and More in Brook Park.

Cara and she had become closer than ever since Grace had been dating Johnny, but had barely spoken to each other since Charlie's funeral. So, when Cara had invited her to an impromptu get-together at Joanne's house for dinner, Grace had offered to pick up the food.

Johnny, who was stuck at the gym training a client, had planned to meet them after at his mom's house. What had made the last minute gathering even more interesting to Grace was Cara's mention that Coop would be there as well, and she couldn't wait to find out why the pitcher was back in

Cleveland while the rest of his team was still in Oakland.

At first, Grace had assumed that Jason was messing with her when he

called because his story about Mick being a fugitive on the run seemed far too

absurd to believe. However, Jason's solemn demeanor as he reassured her that

had wished he was just playing a bad joke told her otherwise.

"I really need you to go to my mom's house right away," Jason

instructed.

"I'm already on my way," Grace replied without hesitation as she

immediately began the five minute drive from Kicker's to Joanne's place.

"You don't think Mick would actually go there, do you?"

"I doubt it," Jason said in response. "But, when I tried to call

Clarence, he didn't answer his phone and that's strange because-"

"Clarence *always* answers his phone," Grace said, finishing Jason's

sentence.

Grace knew Clarence as well as anyone and it was highly unusual for

him to not answer his phone, especially when on duty with his biggest client.

In fact, one of the first demands he made of Grace after she began working for

CW Security Solutions was to always be available by phone when on the clock, no matter what. He had even given her a portable battery charger to have with her at all times in the event her cell phone died.

"I already called my mom and gave her the heads-up to lock the doors and everything, just in case. That's when she told me that Cara, Coop, and Clarence were there too, so I immediately tried calling Clarence," Jason recalled before he added with a slight laugh, "I didn't even think to ask why the hell Coop was back in Cleveland."

"Trust me, I feel you on that last part," Grace chuckled as she sped down Sylvia Drive, which would take her directly to Joanne's street a few blocks down the road.

"It's probably nothing," Jason said in regards to Clarence not answering his call, but he felt as if he was trying to convince himself as much as Grace.

"Where are you at, anyway?" Grace asked.

"I'm back at the precinct," Jason replied. "The U.S. Marshals have a team here, and we are trying to quarterback the entire operation from a central location as best we can. So far, we haven't had much luck finding Mick other than an old lady who said that someone matching Mick's description had

flashed his badge and forced her out of her car not far from his house. We still

have yet to locate that vehicle, but at least we have something..."

"This is insane. Is there anyone else you need me to contact?" Grace

asked. "What about Erica and Gabby?"

"I actually had them come to the precinct earlier today, just to be

safe," Jason answered. "And we already spoke to Mick's ex wife, Zoey."

"Gotcha," Grace acknowledged. "Listen, I'm almost at your mom's

street. I'll give you a call as soon as I make sure everything is kosher."

"Sounds good," Jason replied and then added, "I really appreciate you

doing this, Grace..."

"My pleasure," Grace replied. "Talk to you soon..."

Grace ended the call as she turned right onto Slater Drive. While

Joanne's street was actually located one street past Slater on Gilmere Drive,

the two streets were essentially connected in the form of an elongated "U",

with Cynthia Drive serving as a small connection at the base of the two.

Grace had visited the Knox house enough over the past year to be

aware that the two streets were connected, but those unfamiliar with the neighborhood would likely have no idea that a second route to Joanne's house existed. By turning down Slater, Grace had given herself a tactical advantage in the event there was a reason to be concerned.

It had become quite dark outside as Grace slowly followed the bend where Cynthia turned into Gilmere, but with the help of the streetlights, she could still make out Clarence's Cadillac Escalade, which was parked about 500 feet ahead on the side of the road.

At first, Grace was relieved to see Coop and Cara, who appeared to be standing in the road alongside Clarence's Escalade. However, once she observed the hulking pitcher's body language a little more closely, that relief turned into fear as he appeared to be shielding Cara from something inside the SUV.

Grace resisted the urge to punch the gas and race in their direction. Instead, she slowly pulled over and parked along the street about five houses down from where Clarence was and turned the ignition off.

She used her key to unlock the glove box and retrieved her Glock 9 millimeter semi-automatic pistol, checked to make sure that there was a round in the chamber, and used her phone to call Clarence.

*Late Life*

As the phone rang, Grace continued to keep her eyes fixated on the scene up ahead, which is when she observed Joanne Knox standing near the front door of her house. Though it was too dark for Grace to be certain, it appeared that the recently widowed Joanne's demeanor was anything but relaxed.

After multiple rings, Clarence's phone went to voicemail. She was just about to call Jason back to inform him that something was definitely not right when she witnessed the Escalade's driver side door open.

The overwhelming sense of relief that she had felt upon seeing Clarence exit the SUV was soon replaced by fear as the back door to the Escalade opened up seconds later and a man got out.

It was Mick.. and in each hand he held a gun.

# 55

Mick knew that he had to act the moment that he saw Joanne Knox step outside her front door. While the fact that she had spoken to Jason and had stepped outside to warn the others had made matters bad enough, they only became worse once she had realized that Mick was sitting in the back seat.

"Shit!" Mick exclaimed in frustration at the realization that he would have to come up with yet another plan, and fast.

"Let's think about this, Mick," Clarence said in as calm a manner as possible. He knew that they were at a crossroads and hoped that he could use the opportunity to talk Mick out of doing something irrational. "I don't know what's going on that led up to this moment, and none of that matters to me, Mick. I just don't want to see anyone get hurt…"

"Shut the hell up!" Mick hissed as he poked the back of Clarence's neck with his gun. "Save your bullshit if you really don't want anyone to get hurt."

"Okay, okay," Clarence replied in a relaxed tone. "Just tell me what you want me to do, Mick."

Mick's eyes darted between Clarence, the young couple, and the matriarch of the Knox family as he weighed his options. It didn't take long for Mick to realize that he really only had one option, and he had to act on it quickly. He grabbed Clarence's gun from the seat next to him and aimed it at Coop and Cara while he continued to press the barrel of his Glock against Clarence's neck.

"Now, here's what we are going to do," Mick began to order, his voice just loud enough so that Coop and Cara could hear him. "Clarence, first you're going to take your cell phone, reach over your back shoulder, and drop it onto the floor by my feet."

"Okay," Clarence said as he held his phone over his shoulder and then let it fall to the floor.

"Good. Now, in just a few seconds you're going to exit the truck, which you *will* keep running, and walk towards the house," Mick instructed Clarence before he directed his attention to Coop and Cara. "Coop, once I get out of the vehicle, you are going to follow Clarence and then the two of you are going to lie down, face-first on the grass in the front yard. You're both going to stay there until you see us pull away."

"Us?" Coop asked.

"Do you really think that I'm going to leave here alone?" Mick laughed incredulously. "So much for dispelling the whole 'All jocks are dumb' thing… helluva game last night, by the way…"

"You're insane!" Coop growled as he felt Cara's arms wrap around him from behind.

"Perhaps," Mick mused. "But, the bottom line is that she's going with me and you two are going to lie in the grass until I'm gone or I'll put a bullet in her pretty little face…"

Clarence, who had sensed the rage in Coop building to a crescendo, decided to step in before the ballplayer could do anything rash and said, "Coop, just do as he says, okay? I promise nothing bad will happen, alright?"

Coop shot a look at his bodyguard, whom he couldn't believe was actually giving in to the madman. However, once he saw Clarence's gaze, there was something in his eyes that told Coop not to worry.

"It's going to be okay, Coop," Clarence reiterated as he looked in his rearview mirror. He then slowly opened his door and exited the vehicle. As he cautiously walked past Coop, he gave him a wink.

Coop didn't have time to dissect what Clarence's wink meant because Mick had opened his door and began to exit the Escalade, both guns aimed in their direction, as he instructed, "Okay, Cara, now let your man-child go so he can follow Clarence."

"Actually, Mick, I can't let that happen," Clarence said as he quickly pivoted and placed himself between Mick and the clients that he had sworn to protect.

"I swear to God, I'll shoot all of you if you don't get your ass over there," Mick seethed as he tucked Clarence's gun in the waistband of his jeans while keeping his own firearm trained on the trio.

"You can have the truck," Clarence said calmly as he nodded toward his Escalade, "But, you're going to have to take it alone."

Mick felt the panic inside his brain surge as the realization that he had lost control of the entire situation crept in. He quickly glanced around at the nearby houses to see if any of Joanne's neighbors had heard the commotion. While he didn't see anyone observing the confrontation, Mick knew that someone could have already dialed 9-1-1 to report a man with a gun in the street.

Time was running out.

The sound of police sirens in the distance only increased the anxiety that had already blanketed his psyche. Mick looked at the SUV, which was still running, and decided that he had no other choice than to hop in and drive away - even if it meant that he did so by himself.

Before he could even take a step in the direction of the awaiting vehicle, Mick heard a woman's voice shout from behind him, "Put the gun down, Mick! Now!"

Mick immediately pivoted and saw before him a woman that he had known for years, beginning when she was a police officer working under him at the 1st District, and more recently as one of Clarence's employees at CW Security Solutions. He wasn't sure how she had managed to sneak up on him, nor did he have time to question it because Grace Brooks stood just ten feet away in a tactical firing stance, her 9 millimeter semi-automatic pistol aimed directly at him.

"I said, put the gun down, Mick!" Grace ordered again, seemingly unphased by the fact that Mick had pointed his gun back at her.

Clarence, taking advantage of the new development, maintained his position as a shield for Coop and Cara while he slowly began to walk backwards and usher the couple away from the standoff. Mick, who remained with his gun trained on Grace, didn't seem to notice or care.

"No way," Mick said, rejecting the order from his former subordinate.

"I called the police and they're already on their way, Mick," Grace warned. "I know you hear those sirens, Mick. There's nowhere to go, so just put... the gun... down!"

Mick could hear the sirens getting closer as he tried his best to figure a way out of the mess that he had put himself in. He began to question why he had taken such a big risk by going to Joanne's house instead of just taking the truck he had bought and driven it as far away from Cleveland as possible.

Before he could dwell on his missteps any longer, a man's voice cut through the night from the direction of a neighboring house as it bellowed, "What the hell is going on out here?"

The unexpected interruption had caused Grace to take a brief glance in the direction of the man, who was wearing a white tank top and a pair of pajama pants as he peered at the group from his front door.

Mick, who had not taken his eyes off of Grace, used the opportunity to fire off two shots from his gun in her direction.

*Pop! Pop!*

Grace, despite the shots that had just been fired in her direction, remained in her firing stance and squeezed off three rounds in return.

*Pop! Pop! Pop!*

All three shots struck Mick, two in his chest and one in his abdomen, and sent him immediately to the pavement. The exchange had happened so fast that none of the witnesses, including the man who had yelled from his house, could do anything other than watch in disbelief at the scene that had unfolded before them.

*Late Life*

As Mick writhed in pain on the ground, fighting to survive, he wasn't sure why he had decided at the last second to purposely direct his aim just far enough away from what should have been his intended target.

But, he had, as both bullets had come just inches from striking Grace. Perhaps, Mick thought as he felt his life begin to slip away, it was the Siren who had made him spare Grace's life.

It was the Siren's call that had first led him to kill, but unlike Odysseus in Homer's epic tale, Mick did not have a faithful crew willing to take him away from her tempting song.

Mick could hear her song grow stronger as the blood began to enter his lungs in place of the oxygen that he desperately needed to survive. Just as he had been wrong in assuming that he would never be caught for the murders of Vivian and Dolly, Mick realized that he had also made a fatal error by trusting the call of his Siren.

Just as her two ancient predecessors had done to the sailors who failed to ignore their song, Mick's Siren had composed a melody that would eventually kill anyone who had allowed themselves to succumb to her torturous tune.

As Mick took his final breath, he could hear her song finally begin to fade into the same darkness from which it came.

*Late Life*

# 56

Clarence glanced at his rearview mirror and smiled at the sight of Coop and Cara, hand in hand, as they sat in the back seat of his Escalade as it made its way towards Burke Lakefront Airport. He had thought about divulging the secret that he had been keeping from them for the entire duration of the ride, but realized that the couple had already been through enough in recent days, so his secret would have to remain that way for the time being.

It had been three days since they had witnessed Grace Brooks fatally shoot Mick, and the aftermath of his death brought with it evidence that Mick had not only murdered Dolly, but had also been responsible for the killing of Vivian Tong.

It was when authorities had discovered a laminated West Virginia driver's license with Mick's image on it that they learned how the disgraced police commander was the true identity of the infamous Eugene Lankford. While the authorities would likely never know that Mick had blackmailed the deceased owner of Buddy's Speakeasy, Vance Gold, to keep his mouth shut during the investigation into his former employee's death, what they did know was that Eugene Lankford would never kill again.

Grace Brooks, who was legally permitted to carry a firearm in her role as a bodyguard for CW Security Solutions, was immediately cleared of any possible criminal charges for the shooting as it was ruled an act of self-defense by the investigators who had arrived at the scene minutes after Mick's death.

While Clarence knew that Grace was as mentally tough as anyone he had ever known, he did have concerns over how the long-term impact of the shooting might affect her. She had remained her usual self in the days since the shooting, but Clarence had also encouraged her to speak to a professional to help her work through the emotions that were likely to come down the road. He had scheduled a lunch meeting with her later that day, not only to gauge how she was doing, but also to discuss the secret that he had been keeping from everyone - including her.

"It's not too late to turn around and head back to the Westcott, you know," Coop reminded Cara as the SUV pulled into the entrance of Burke Lakefront, where a private jet was waiting to take him back to the west coast to rejoin his teammates.

Coop didn't have to inform the club of his involvement the night of Mick's death, thanks to the multiple media reports which had instantly surfaced showing him at the crime scene, but he called them the next morning, regardless. The General Manager of the club had told Coop to stay in Cleveland for as long as he needed to, even if it meant missing his last start of the season. The team had dropped its next three games after Coop's miraculous outing, and their chances of making the postseason had evaporated with the losses.

"I told you that I don't have to go," Coop reiterated as Clarence pulled onto the tarmac. "Tonight's game doesn't mean anything. The club doesn't care if I stay here."

Cara, who had actually been the one who had insisted on Coop rejoining the team, replied, "Yes, you do. You've worked so hard to get back out there and you just pitched the best game of your career. I'm not going to let you miss your next start; even if it's meaningless to the team, it's not meaningless to you. I know it isn't…"

As much as Cara had wanted Coop to stay in Cleveland, she was also tired of feeling like their relationship had caused enough issues for his career in recent weeks. Between her father's death, her reaction to the CMZ article, and the chaos involving Mick, it was shocking to her that he had pitched so well despite all of those obstacles.

"Why don't you come with me then?" Coop asked as the SUV came to a stop just feet from the awaiting jet.

"As much as I would love to, I can't," Cara replied. "My family really needs me here. My mom is still a mess in regards to my dad, let alone the fact that she witnessed someone get shot to death, and I know that Jason is grieving the entire situation with Mick, despite him acting like everything's fine."

While Cara knew that her family was dealing with the trauma of recent events, she also was still trying to process everything herself. While she had watched her father take his last breath, seeing Mick do the same after being shot three times right in front of her had kept her from sleeping the first

362

two nights after. Cara realized that she needed to be around her family just as much as they needed her.

"Are you just gonna sit up there and be quiet?" Coop asked, directing his words at Clarence. "C'mon man, you always have advice for me all the times I'm not even asking for it, but I really need your help here."

Clarence chuckled and replied, "I'll tell you what I've told you before…"

"Just do what she says," Coop laughed as he finished the sentence. "Thanks for the help…"

"I think they're waiting for you, Coop," Clarence said, referring to the team staffer who was impatiently checking his watch at the base of the jet's staircase.

"You better get going," Cara said as she fought to hold back the tears that were certain to come as soon as Coop exited the vehicle.

"I'm gonna miss you," Coop said as he brushed a loose strand of hair away from her cheek.

"Just call me when you land, okay?" Cara asked as she continued to keep her composure.

"I will," he said before adding, "and after that I'm fixin' to see if I can't throw myself another one of those perfect games tonight. I kinda liked that the last time, so I figure I'll give it another whirl..."

Coop's words brought a smile to Cara's face and she said, "I love you, Cooper Madison."

"I love you more," he replied.

The two embraced and Cara felt the emotions that she had been trying to keep at bay surge. She kissed him on the lips and said, "You better get going..."

"I feel like there's more that I want to say though," Coop, who was now fighting back tears of his own, said as he pressed his head against hers.

Just as she and Coop had said hundreds of times to each other throughout the course of their relationship, Cara placed her index finger over his lips and whispered, "Nothing..."

Coop smiled upon hearing the one word that would always be their favorite way to end a conversation, even when there was more that could have been said.

"Nothing..." he replied.

A few minutes later, as Clarence drove away from the airport, he asked Cara, "Are you sure that you don't want to stay and watch the jet take off?"

Cara, who by this point had let her emotions completely overcome her, replied through her tears, "No thank you. I just want to go back to my mom's house."

Clarence simply nodded in return, and as he drove away from the airport, he took a moment and reminisced about the day he first met Coop and Cara. He had been a part of their lives since their relationship was in its infancy, and he had grown to love them as if they were part of his own family.

*Late Life*

# 57

Joanne Knox wiped a tear away as she admired the silver dollar that she had just placed on top of her late husband's headstone at Holy Cross Cemetery, which was located just a few miles from the house they had called home for over two decades.

Charlie Knox loved silver dollars, specifically the version known as the American Silver Eagle, and he had been known to always have at least a couple in his pocket at all times. While he never made a habit of using the coins as a form of currency, that didn't mean that he held on to them either.

In fact, the tellers at Huntington Bank had always made sure to have at least a few dozen on hand for Charlie during his weekly trips to their branch when he would replenish his supply.

*Late Life*

Like many people bound to a wheelchair, Charlie had grown
accustomed to the regular interactions with curious children who would often
ask him questions about how he ended up that way. On many occasions,
Joanne herself had witnessed those encounters, most of which resulted in an
embarrassed parent apologizing for their child's indiscreet line of questioning.

"Oh, no need to apologize," Charlie would typically respond as he
reached into his pocket to retrieve one of the silver dollars. He then would
hold the shiny coin up for the child to see and in a serious tone he would say,
"You see, I need this chair because I have so many of these special coins, and
they're so heavy in my pockets that I couldn't possibly walk around with them
all day."

Despite the fact that she had seen his routine many times in the years
since his accident, Joanne would always marvel at how captivated the child
would become at the sight of the rare coin.

Once he knew that he had the child's full attention, Charlie would ask,
"I'll tell you what, do you think you can help me with my coin problem? If
you promise to listen to your mom and dad, I'll give you this coin to keep. Do
you think that you could do that for me? It would be a big help…"

368

Joanne couldn't remember an occasion where the child refused the terms of Charlie's proposal, though sometimes they would look to their mom or dad first for approval before accepting the coin.

"Why do you do that?" Joanne had asked after the first time that she had witnessed the interaction.

"I suppose that I just want them to know that people who look like me have some sort of value to add to their lives, even if it's just a dollar's worth," Charlie had replied.

Joanne had never forgotten his words, and as she continued to sort through all the possessions that Charlie had left behind in the days since his death, she discovered that he'd stashed away dozens of the coins in various places around the house. She had decided in recent days that she would always carry a few in her purse in the event that she found herself in a position to add value to someone's life, even if it was just a dollar's worth.

"I know that you're watching down on all of us," Joanne said as she stared at the headstone before her. "And I know that you heard my prayer the other night. I was so scared, Charlie, but I could feel your presence with me. With all of us…"

*Late Life*

Joanne took a deep breath, and with a trembling voice said, "I miss you so much, Charlie. I'm so worried that I'm not going to be able to do this without you…"

At first, Joanne had assumed that her mind was playing tricks on her when she heard a woman's voice call out from behind her, "Charlie, get back here!"

However, when she heard the voice repeat itself again, she turned around and saw a young mother chasing after a little boy who had decided to turn the cemetery into his own personal playground.

The boy, who appeared to be no more than 6 years of age, had managed to climb on top of a headstone just a few feet from where Joanne was standing. He had red hair and was wearing a Spiderman shirt that reminded her of a similar one that Jason wore as a child.

"I'm Spiderman!" the boy announced as he jumped off the top of the headstone, landing just a few steps from Joanne.

"Charles Benjamin Fletterick, you get back here this instant!" the mother yelled as she closed the gap on her evasive son, who by this point had stopped moving long enough to stare at Charlie's headstone.

370

"Hey, that's my name!" the boy exclaimed after recognizing the familiar letters that had been chiseled into Charlie's marker.

"Is that so?" Joanne asked as she kneeled down next to him.

"Yup," the boy said proudly. "It's spelled C-H-A-R-L-E-S. That spells Charles, but I like to be called Charlie…"

The boy's mother, who by this point had finally caught up to her son, looked at Joanne and in a flustered tone said, "I'm so sorry, ma'am. I was putting flowers on my mother's grave for her birthday and the next thing I knew he was off and running."

"Oh, there's no need," Joanne said, who politely dismissed the woman's apology with a wave of her hand before adding, "I have three boys of my own, though it was my daughter who was typically the runner."

"What's that?" the little boy said as he pointed at the coin on top of Charlie's headstone.

"Charles!" his mom gasped, obviously mortified that her son had not only scaled a gravestone, but had also now begun to question a grieving stranger.

"Oh, it's fine," Joanne reassured the young mother before asking the boy, "Would you like to see it?"

The boy nodded yes and Joanne rose to her feet, retrieved the coin, and brought it back to show him.

"You see, Charlie, my husband absolutely loved these coins," Joanne said as she held the coin out so the boy could see it. "This one is called an American Silver Eagle dollar and he would give them out to little kids just like you, but only if they promised to listen to their parents."

The boys eyes widened as he gazed upon the shiny coin.

"If I give you this coin, will you promise me that you'll listen to your mom the rest of the day?" Joanne asked.

"Yes," the boy replied, nodding enthusiastically as his eyes remained fixated on the silver dollar.

"Well then, here you go," Joanne said as she handed the coin to his eager hands.

"That is so nice of her, isn't it Charlie?" His mother then prompted, "What do you say when someone gives you something nice?"

"Thank you," the boy said as he examined the treasure.

372

"You are very welcome, Charlie," Joanne replied. "Now, don't forget what I said about listening to your mother, okay?"

"I won't," the boy promised as he held the coin up to his eyes for a closer examination.

"Thank you, again," his mom said. "And, I'm very sorry for your loss. He must've been an amazing man."

Joanne smiled and replied, "Yes, he certainly was…"

As the boy and his mother walked away, Joanne felt for the first time since her husband's passing that maybe she would be able to find value in her new life after all.

Even if it was just one dollar at a time.

*Late Life*

# 58

Clarence, upon seeing Grace enter the lounge area of Bucci's Italian Restaurant, motioned to get her attention from his seat at the booth in the far corner of his favorite Italian eatery in Berea, Ohio.

"How are you holding up?" Clarence asked his top employee as she took a seat across from him. It was the first time he had seen her in person since the night of the shooting.

"I'm hanging in there," Grace replied. "I finally got some sleep last night for the first time since, well, you know…"

They paused as a waitress came over and took their drink orders.

"I'm sure that it's been weighing on you quite a bit," Clarence acknowledged. "What's important is that you know that what you did was everything that you've been trained to do. I hope you know that, Grace."

"I do," Grace sighed. "Trust me, I've replayed the whole scenario a million times in my head trying to figure out if it could've been avoided had I just done something differently. Maybe if I had just waited until the police arrived to confront him, things would've turned out differently…"

Clarence nodded with empathy as he listened. While it broke his heart to know that she was going through the natural progression that anyone in her position would, he was just as equally proud of her actions that night. Even though he couldn't say anything that would make things better, he knew that it was his job to make sure that she understood how appreciative he was that she had put herself in harm's way in order to protect not only their clients, but also him.

"You're right," he replied. "You could've stayed back and waited for the police to arrive, and nobody would've blamed you if you had. That being said, Mick knew that he was in a desperate situation and who knows what he would have done had you not confronted him."

"I know…" Grace agreed. "But, I can't help but wonder if I had waited that maybe he'd still be alive."

"Perhaps," Clarence acknowledged. "He might be, but maybe I wouldn't. Same goes for Coop, Cara, and Joanne."

As much as Grace had replayed the events of that fateful evening in her head, she had obviously come to the conclusion that had she not stepped in, Mick very well could have harmed the others. However, hearing Clarence say it made it that much more real to her and she began to feel tears well up in her eyes.

"That's been the one thing that I know I wouldn't have been able to live with had it happened," Grace speculated.

"I know," Clarence replied in a reassuring tone. "And even if Mick had just jumped in my Escalade and driven off alone, I'm pretty sure that he would've met the same fate. Guys in Mick's position don't just surrender. He was either going to get away or die trying. The way I choose to look at it is that had he been cornered by the police, he might've taken an officer or two with him as he made his final stand. Worse yet, an innocent bystander might've been killed, too. So, you have to take all of that into consideration as you try and make sense of what happened."

"I suppose you're right." Grace's voice had become soft with emotion as the tears streamed down her cheeks.

Clarence handed her his napkin and added, "It's okay to feel this way, Grace, and while I wish that I could say something that would make it all go away, I can't. Do you want to know the best advice I ever was given after the first time that I had a similar experience?"

Grace, as she wiped the tears away from her face, nodded yes. Clarence waited until after the waitress brought their drinks to the table.

"It was during one of my first years on the job, and I had been involved in a vehicular pursuit. My partner and I had pulled a guy over for speeding, but after running his license, we learned from dispatch that he had a warrant out on him for his involvement in a gang shooting," Clarence recalled. "He must've known that we were going to find out about the warrant because he took off on us while we were still in the cruiser. I mean, this guy tore outta there like a bat out of hell."

"Oh man," Grace replied. "I used to always hold my breath when I'd pull someone over whose info came back showing a warrant. Thankfully, none of them ever took off on me."

"Well, this guy had other plans," Clarence chuckled at the recollection. "So, I'm behind the wheel that day, and my partner and I radio it in that he's on the move and begin our pursuit. It was the middle of the afternoon on a beautiful Saturday and there were people all over the place."

"Where were you guys at when you pulled him over?" Grace asked.

"Over by Kamm's Corner," Clarence replied, referring to the historic west side neighborhood in Cleveland. "He was headed eastbound on Lorain Avenue."

"Oh no, I bet there were pedestrians all over the place."

"Everywhere," Clarence confirmed. "And this guy is going about 80 through the intersection at Rocky River Drive. He narrowly missed two people crossing the street as he blew through a red light. We maintained our pursuit, lights on and sirens blaring, hoping that would help alert anyone else near the street."

"That's the hardest part when you're in pursuit," Grace sighed. "You not only have to worry about keeping up with the car you're after, but you also have to make sure nobody else gets clipped."

"Ain't that the truth," Clarence agreed. "So, this guy's still flying down Lorain. Thankfully, a lot of the cars up ahead of us realize what's going down and most of them begin to pull over toward the side of the road. That is, with the exception of a guy driving a dump truck coming from the opposite direction right at the car we're chasing."

"Oh no," Grace said in response. "Please tell me he didn't…"

"Oh, he did," Clarence said, shaking his head in disbelief. "The dump truck driver told us afterwards that he had decided that he was going to help us out and cut the guy off by turning his truck into the other lane to block the road. Our guy tries to slam on the brakes, but it was too late and he slammed right into the undercarriage of the truck. He wasn't wearing his seatbelt and went straight through his front windshield. He was killed instantly…"

"Oh no, that's awful!" Grace gasped as she covered her mouth with her hand in disbelief.

"To make matters worse, we find out later that he had two little kids," Clarence sighed. "Even though he was obviously mixed up in some bad things, he was still just a 22 year old kid himself, and now his babies were without their father."

Grace shook her head solemnly and said, "I'm so sorry you had to experience that, Clarence."

"I appreciate that," Clarence replied. "But, the reason I'm sharing it with you is that in the days that followed I replayed the scenario hundreds of times in my head, second-guessing every decision I made and wondered if I had just done something differently that the young man would still be alive. Thankfully, my commander made me go see a therapist who specialized in dealing with cops who had experienced a traumatic event on the job. I didn't want to go, but I was told that I wasn't allowed back on the job until I did, and now I am forever grateful that I did."

"What did the therapist say to you that helped you through it?" Grace asked.

"He told me that the only way to move forward was to accept the fact that I could only focus my energy on what actually happened, as opposed to what *could* have happened. He said that while there wasn't anything that I could do to bring that young man's life back, that I could deal with the emotions that I was dealing with as a result of what had happened. He made me realize that it was okay for me to feel everything that I was and gave me strategies to help address those issues."

"That makes a whole lot of sense to me, especially right now," Grace admitted.

"I still have his card, you know," Clarence said as he produced a worn beige business card from his wallet and handed it to Grace. "I really think you should give him a call. I hope you don't mind, but I already contacted him and explained your situation and he told me that he'd be happy to talk to you. I told him to bill me…"

"Thank you, Clarence," Grace said as she looked at the card. "I think that I'll take him up on that."

"I'm happy to hear you say that," Clarence replied. "Because, I'm going to really need you to be in the best state of mind when you take over the company for me."

At first, Clarence's words didn't seem to sink in for Grace, who was still looking down at the card in her hands. However, a few seconds later she looked up at her boss with a surprised expression and asked, "Take over the company? What are you talking about, Clarence?"

Clarence smiled, took a deep breath, and replied, "I've been contemplating retiring for some time now. In fact, had we not taken on Coop as a client, it probably would've happened sooner. The reality is that I'm ready to finally give Evelynn the life that we have always dreamed of having once we were both ready for that next chapter. That is, if you think that you're ready to take on that kind of responsibility. I know that you've been training really hard for your MMA fight in December, and I promise that I'll make sure that you have all the time you need to make that dream a reality."

"Clarence," a shocked Grace began, "I don't know what to say. I mean, I'm beyond flattered that you would trust me to do this, but I don't know anything about running a company."

"You'll learn," Clarence reassured her. "We'll take this transition as slowly as we need to until you're ready, and maybe by sometime in January you'll be prepared to take the reigns. Even then, I'll still be involved in an advisory role, but I just can't commit myself to the day-to-day responsibilities that come with running the business."

"Do you really think I'll be any good at this?" Grace asked as her mind raced.

"I wouldn't be asking you if I didn't," Clarence chuckled. "I have all the confidence in the world in you, Grace. I know you'll do amazingly well, and I'll always be there to help guide you through any challenges as they arise. Besides, this will be a pretty sizeable raise for you when you officially become the CEO of C.W. Security Solutions. You don't have to let me know today. Take as much time as you need to think it over."

"I'll do it," Grace replied with confidence. "I don't need any time to think it over. I would be honored to accept this responsibility."

"Well then," Clarence said as he reached across the table to shake Grace's hand. "Congratulations, CEO Brooks."

"Does Coop or Cara know about this decision yet?" Grace asked after she shook his hand.

Clarence took a deep breath and exhaled before giving his response.

"No, not yet. Besides you, the only person who knows is my wife. But, I will be breaking the news to them soon, when the time is right."

Clarence was well aware that there never would be a "right" time to let them know that the man that they had entrusted with their lives over the past year would no longer be watching over them on a daily basis. However, he also knew that they had held Grace in the highest of regards during her time with the couple, and he was confident that once the initial shock wore off, they would be understanding of his decision.

"I do have just one more question," Grace said, letting her words hang.

"What's that?" Clarence replied.

"You saw me in your rearview mirror that night didn't you?" Grace asked. "I mean, you had to have known I was there. It's the only explanation that I can come up with to explain why you were so confident when you refused Mick's orders to get in the truck."

Clarence, who had anticipated this question from his protégé ever since that fateful night, chose to respond with only a smile.

"Oh, you're just gonna leave me hangin' like that?" Grace pressed.

Clarence maintained his smile and gave her a wink.

*Late Life*

# 59

"Thank you for doing this," Hannah said to Jason later that evening as soon as she saw her director at Channel One News indicate that they were off the air. "I'm sure that it wasn't easy for you to talk about, especially on live television."

"It wasn't," Jason admitted. "But, I'm glad that I could help. Talking about it has actually helped me deal with everything, to be honest."

The two had just finished an exclusive interview regarding Mick, which had sent shock waves throughout the entire Cleveland Division of Police. Hannah had approached Jason the day before and asked him if he would be interested in doing the live broadcast.

She had explained to him that her producer at the station was pressuring her to do an interview about the disgraced police commander and that they had insisted that she used her relationship with Jason to convince him to agree to it. If he declined, she had informed him when they spoke, her producer had instructed her to get the highest-ranking officer that would agree to do it.

Jason, after receiving approval from Chief Lawson, agreed to do the sit down. If anyone was going to tell Mick's story, he figured it should be him.

Per Chief Lawson's request, Jason avoided going into any details that could possibly hamper the ongoing investigation into Mick's past, which meant that he had informed Hannah that he wasn't allowed to discuss anything involving Vivian Tong. He did, however, discuss the parts of Dolly's murder that he had been cleared to speak upon. He was also given the green light to give the basics of what had led to Mick being shot, as long as he only identified the shooter as a, "private security officer who had acted within her legal rights to fire upon the suspect in self-defense."

"So, how are you holding up?" Hannah had asked as a staff member helped Jason remove his lapel microphone.

"I'd be lying if I said that I wasn't dealing with some heavy stuff," Jason sighed. "But, I'm supposed to meet with my therapist tomorrow. I've been seeing him ever since the Ernie Page case when Clarence had given me his name. I've been going pretty regularly ever since."

"Good for you," Hannah expressed as she placed a comforting hand on his shoulder. "It's important to talk to someone. Trust me, I've been seeing a therapist for years myself. This line of work can really mess with your head."

"I bet," Jason agreed.

"I hate to change the subject," Hannah began, "But, one of my sources at the department said that you are in line to succeed Mick as the Commander of the 1st District. Let me be the first to congratulate you."

"You and your sources," Jason laughed. "I have been approached by the chief in regards to the promotion, but I haven't made a decision. I haven't even spoken to Erica about it yet. While it would certainly be nice to make the jump, I'm not sure that I could sit in Mick's old office every day."

"I understand," Hannah replied. "How are Erica and Gabby doing with everything that's happened?"

"Thankfully, Gabby is blissfully unaware. I know at some point we will have to explain to her that Mick is gone, which will be tough because she thought of him as an uncle of sorts," Jason acknowledged. "As far as Erica goes, let's just say that I couldn't have asked for a better wife if I tried. She's been amazing the past few days. Gabby is staying at my mom's house tonight so that Erica and I can spend some time together."

"You're lucky to have someone like that," Hannah stated. "And, I'm sure that she would say that she's pretty lucky to have someone like you, too."

"Depends on the day," Jason mused. "How about you? Any luck on the dating scene these days? The last time I asked you if there was someone special in your life you just told me that your last date was with Jack Daniels…"

"Oh, I had to break it off with good ole Jack. He was always fun to hang out with, but he typically would give me a headache the next morning," Hannah said in jest. She then smiled and said, "Actually, I'm leaving from here to meet someone I've been seeing."

"Oh yeah?" Jason replied. "Who's the lucky guy?"

"His name is Eric Gulden," Hannah answered.

"Do you need me to run his name through the system?" Jason offered, only half-joking.

"Stop it!" Hannah laughed. "He's actually a first grade teacher in Lakewood, so I'm pretty sure he passed an FBI background check before he was allowed to teach there."

"First grade, huh?" Jason replied, surprised.

"Isn't that adorable?" Hannah asked, rhetorically. "Get this, he played tight end at John Carroll and coaches football at LHS, so he's like this big teddy bear."

"Well, I'm happy for you," Jason declared. "You deserve someone amazing."

"Awe, that's so sweet of you to say," Hannah replied. "And, so far, he seems pretty amazing."

"I better get going," Jason said after looking at his watch. "I made reservations at Pier W and I promised Erica that I wouldn't be late, for once."

"Don't let me be the reason to keep you from breaking your promise," Hannah said as she gave Jason a friendly hug goodbye.

Jason had begun to make his exit from the studio when he stopped, turned around, and said to Hannah, "Hey, Miss LaMarca, can you do me a favor?"

"What's that?" she replied.

"Make sure that I'm always at the top of your secret list of sources within the department, okay?" he said in a sincere tone.

"I wouldn't have it any other way, Detective," Hannah replied, returning the sentiment. "And don't worry, when I do visit, I'll make sure to bring the coffee…"

Jason smiled in return and exited the studio. While he knew that it would be a long time before he could possibly digest everything that had occurred over the past week, one thing that he was sure of was that he was grateful for all the people in his life that would help him get through it.

# 60

Clarence had just parked his SUV in front of the Westcott Hotel after picking Cara up from her mom's house, where he had taken her after leaving Coop at the airport. Cara gave him a hug and thanked him for helping her smooth things over with her niece.

Cara had felt awful about canceling her trip to the zoo with Gabby earlier that week and wanted to make up for it once she had learned that her niece would be spending the night at Joanne's.

In an effort to show Gabby that she was sorry, Cara had brought her mom's make-up kit out and let her niece give her a makeover. Since Gabby had made her keep the make-up on, which was less than flattering, Cara looked as ridiculous as she felt as she entered the Westcott.

It was a small price to pay, Cara thought, to know that her niece had not held any animosity against her for the zoo trip that didn't happen.

As the concierge at the Westcott, Simon Craig, took in the sight of Cara's painted face as she entered the lobby, he couldn't prevent the look of utter shock that had come over his face.

"What? Don't you think that I look good?" Cara had laughed, thoroughly embracing the situation. "Gabby gave me a makeover…"

"If by good you mean a circus clown who tried applying his makeup on a roller coaster," Simon replied in a snarky manner as he looked as if he was staring at a dead body.

"Hey," Cara said, ignoring his joke, "I'm going to head upstairs and clean this masterpiece off before Coop's game comes on. Are you still coming up to watch with me?"

"Only if you promise to never, and I mean *neh-ver*, let that little girl do that to your precious face again," Simon replied, doing his best to sound sincere before he let out a laugh.

394

"Okay, okay, I do," Cara promised. "Just give me like ten minutes to get cleaned up. We can order some food from Stucky's, if you'd like. I'm starving!"

"You might need more than ten minutes," Simon mused.

"I'll see you soon," Cara said as she made her way to the elevator.

Minutes later, as Cara approached the door to suite 1100, she swore that she had heard the sound of music coming from inside the door of the penthouse. As she opened the door, the sound of Billy Joel's "She's Always a Woman" grew louder and Cara wondered if she had accidentally left the radio on before she left.

Cara wasn't sure if she smelled the aroma of the shrimp boil that emanated from the kitchen before or after she found herself staring at a smiling Coop as he greeted her, but she didn't give it another thought as she immediately threw herself into his muscular frame and began to cry.

"Hey, girl," Coop said as he squeezed her tight and kissed the top of her head.

"What are you doing here?" Cara asked through her tears as she continued to press the side of her face into his chest, praying that she wasn't imagining his presence. "You're supposed to be pitching a game soon!"

"I couldn't bring myself to leave," Coop replied. "Right after I boarded the jet, I told the staffer that I had changed my mind and to call me a cab. So, I came back, hoping to surprise you, but you weren't here."

"I was at my mom's house with Gabby," Cara said, her cheek still firmly planted in the same spot.

"Yeah, Clarence told me when I called him," Coop admitted. "He had asked if I wanted him to tell you that I was home, but I told him to keep it a secret since I was fixin' to make us a special dinner. Simon helped me get all the stuff I needed for a shrimp boil, just like the one I made for you on our first date."

"I thought I smelled shrimp," Cara acknowledged, before the realization that Simon had obviously known that Coop was waiting for her, and he still let her go upstairs with make-up all over her face. "Oh my God, I'm going to kill Simon!"

"Why's that?" Coop said, pretending that he had not noticed the make-up when she entered the room. In reality, Clarence had called him as soon as Cara had entered the Westcott to give him a heads-up about the rudimentary make-over.

Cara slowly pulled her face away from Coop's broad chest, whose shirt now had streaks of colorful mascara on it, pointed to her face and said, "Because of this!"

"Oh, did you try a new shade of eyeliner or something?" Coop asked, keeping up the charade.

"Very funny!" Cara replied as she gave him a playful thump to his chest with her hand.

"Well, despite Miss Gabby's efforts, I still think you look beautiful," Coop said as he smiled and stared into her eyes.

"I know I told you that you should go to your game, but I lied," Cara admitted as the tears started up again. "I cried the entire way to my mom's..."

Coop wiped a tear away from her face and in his deep, southern accent said, "I'm here, and I'm not going anywhere. I love you, Cara..."

*Late Life*

"I love you, too," Cara whispered just before Coop drew her in close and kissed her passionately on the lips.

# Epilogue

"Who would win in a fight? Darth Vader or Kylo Ren?"

Cooper Madison grinned as he pondered the latest of Luke's many questions. His son, like most 9-year-olds, always had a never-ending arsenal of hypothetical queries for his father. Most of them involved Star Wars, Marvel superheroes, or professional athletes… and, naturally, who would win in a fight.

"Well, that depends, I suppose," Coop replied.

"On what?"

"Are we talking about Darth Vader in the *Empire Strikes Back* or Darth Vader in *Return of the Jedi*?"

"Why does *that* even matter?" Luke asked.

"Oh it matters a whole lot, Young Skywalker," Coop answered in his best Darth Vader voice.

"How?"

"Well, in *Empire*, Darth was at his maniacal best. By the end of *Jedi*, he went all soft…"

"What's maniacal mean?" Luke asked.

"I think that you should look it up in the dictionary when we get home," Coop replied.

"What's a dictionary?" Luke quipped, needling his old man.

"It's kinda like that iPad you never put down, only it has pages you can actually turn," Coop chuckled as he looked over at his only child in the passenger seat of the 1996 Dodge Ram.

The truck had been a gift to Coop's late father, Jeffrey, and was the first big purchase that Coop had made after being drafted number one overall in the Major League Draft that same year. Back in 2006, Coop had it fully restored, and more than a decade later, he would still drive it on nice days.

"Looks like your mama beat us home," Coop said as he turned the truck onto a long driveway off of Schady Road in Olmsted Township, a small suburb located just southwest of Cleveland.

As a younger man, Coop would have never imagined that he would live in the same town that his father had been raised in. He had always assumed that he would have retired back home to the Gulf Coast in Pass Christian, Mississippi. However, this was home now, and the main reason for that was standing in the driveway waving in the direction of his truck as he pulled in.

Seeing the former Cara Knox still gave Coop butterflies. Even though she was nearing 40 years of age, she did not look a day over 30. She was wearing a navy tank top and running shorts that perfectly complemented her toned, athletic physique.

The former high school basketball player and track athlete had been blessed with a body that didn't require the three grueling workouts that she put it through each week at Title Boxing Club in nearby Westlake, but Cara was never one to settle for being average in any part of her life.

She attacked everything she did, from being a mother and wife to her career as the owner and CEO of Madison Public Relations, with the same drive and determination that had first attracted Coop to her.

Cara didn't *have* to work. Coop had made more than enough money during his professional baseball career to support the next five generations of Madisons, but it was always very important to her that she had a career to call her own.

Aside from Coop's initial investment to help get her firm started, she had built her company into one of the premier PR firms in the Midwest all on her own. She had even insisted on paying Coop the money from his initial investment back to him, with interest, the moment that she was able to.

"I picked up Angelina's on the way home for dinner," Cara announced as Coop and Luke exited the truck, referring to their favorite local pizza place.

"Well, that sounds almost as good as you look, girl," Coop replied as he approached, smiling. "In fact, you look so good, I'm surprised they didn't give you the pizza for free."

"Who says they didn't?" Cara quipped, coyly.

"You fixin' to make me jealous?" Coop asked as he wrapped his strong arms around her. Despite living up north for as many years as he did down south, his drawl and penchant for southern colloquialisms had resisted any Yankee intervention.

"Did you get the cheesy breadsticks, too?" Luke interrupted as he ran past them towards the front door.

"Hey, boy!" Coop shouted, his deep 'Dad voice' stopping Luke in his tracks. "You come back here and give your mama a hug before you even think about touching that doorknob."

"Yessir," Luke complied as he sheepishly walked over and gave Cara a hug. Even though Coop's son was a northerner by birth, he had been raised to answer his parents the same way that his father had - with respect.

"The breadsticks are on the counter," Cara whispered as she kissed Luke on his cheek.

"Sweet!" Luke exclaimed as he ran towards the house.

"Wash your hands before you touch that food!" Cara called after him.

"Yes, ma'am!" Luke answered over his shoulder before bounding through the front door.

403

"So, Coach, how was practice?" Cara asked as Coop grabbed the bucket of baseballs that were in the bed of his truck.

"Well, we only had one kid cry today, so I'd say it went as well as a final practice before the playoffs could go," Coop sighed playfully.

Just a couple of weeks earlier, it was Luke who had cried in the dugout before practice when he had learned that his dad's old elbow injury had flared up again. The pain, which could have jeopardized the status of the best batting practice pitcher ever to step onto an Olmsted Falls baseball diamond, had thankfully subsided after a few days of ice and rest.

However, just as Coop had promised his son, he did everything in his power to make sure that he was ready to throw BP at practice that night. Mark Patterson, the team's manager, was perhaps the most relieved person on the team, as he had to assume the pitching duties while Coop rested his arm.

Coop loved being an assistant coach. During his playing days, he always figured if he was ever going to become a coach after retirement that he would want to be an assistant, as opposed to the manager of a team. The assistant coaches, regardless of the level of play, typically only had to worry about coaching and executing what the manager had game-planned for them to do. They didn't have to worry about making line-ups, keeping people happy, or any of the other stresses that accompanied being a manager.

"How's the arm feeling?" Cara asked.

"Ask me tomorrow," Coop laughed.

"Make sure you ice it tonight."

"Yes, ma'am," Coop replied. "But not until after I tear into that Angelina's Pizza. I'm hungrier than a tick on a teddy bear."

"Just make sure you wash your hands first, too," Cara chuckled. "Speaking of, I'm going to go make sure young Master Luke didn't forget. He thinks he's smart, that one. Yesterday I caught him just running the water over his hands for a couple seconds without soap."

"That sounds about right," Coop laughed, knowing that he had done the same as a child.

"You boys, I swear," Cara said as she winked before turning and walking towards the house.

Coop stood and admired her as she approached the front door, and just like so many times before, he found himself feeling grateful that Cara was his wife. They had been through so much together ever since she walked into his life thirteen years earlier.

"Hey, girl," Coop called out.

Cara paused, smiling as she heard her husband's familiar greeting, thinking that never got old to hear that "Yankee Drawl" call out after her.

"Yes?" she replied, turning towards him. She knew what he would say next in the same way that she knew the sun would set that evening.

"Nothing…" he said.

"Nothing…"